DATE DUE

AUG 0 2			

A
BOY
LIKE
ASTRID'S
MOTHER

A BOY LIKE ASTRID'S MOTHER

MAE BRISKIN

W·W·NORTON & COMPANY

New York · London

Some of the stories in this collection appeared previously in the following pub-
lications:

"A Boy Like Astrid's Mother," under the title "The Boy Who Was Astrid's
Mother," *Ascent*, Vol. 1, No. 1, 1975, reprinted in *Best American Short
Stories, 1976.* "The Kid," *Western Humanities Review*, Autumn 1976.
"Present Tense," *Western Humanities Review*, Spring 1982, reprinted in
San Francisco Chronicle, April 5, 1987. "Before and After Celeste," *Con-
frontation*, Nos. 25–26, 1983. "Children, Dogs and Dying Men," *Mid-
American Review*, Fall 1983. "Giant Sequoia," *Western Humanities Review*,
Winter 1985. "Theresa McCann and Joe," *Village Advocate*, March 2,
1986, *San Francisco Chronicle*, March 23, 1986, *Chicago Tribune Maga-
zine*, May 4, 1986. "Two Women, One Child" appeared as "Hangin' In,"
Saint Anthony Messenger, January 1987. "Marshall in Rome," *Western
Humanities Review*, Spring 1987. "My Father and Signor Corelli," *St.
Petersburg Times*, July 11, 1987, *Village Advocate*, August 2, 1987, *Albu-
querque Journal Magazine*, August 4, 1987.

Published simultaneously in Canada by Penguin Books Canada Ltd.,
2801 John Street, Markham, Ontario L3R 1B4.
Printed in the United States of America.

The text of this book is composed in Sabon,
with display type set in Korinna Bold.
Composition and manufacturing by
The Maple-Vail Book Manufacturing Group.
Book design by Jacques Chazaud.

First Edition

Library of Congress Cataloging-in-Publication Data

Briskin, Mae, 1924–
A boy like Astrid's mother / Mae Briskin.
p.   cm.
I. Title.
PS3552.R492B6 1988
813'.54—dc19   87–33774
ISBN 0-393-02603-5

W. W. Norton & Company, Inc.
500 Fifth Avenue, New York, N. Y. 10110
W. W. Norton & Company Ltd.
37 Great Russell Street, London WC1B 3NU

1 2 3 4 5 6 7 8 9 0

For my Husband

Herbert B. Briskin

To Daniel Curley,
who published my first story,

John L'Heureux,
who took me into the Stanford Writing Program,

and Dina Viggiano,
who taught me Italian,

My sincere thanks.

Contents

PART TWO

Part One

A Boy
Like
Astrid's Mother

In a box headed "Advertisement" on page four of the paper, was a small photo of a smiling girl. Below it was the message, "Astrid, I miss you. Please contact me. Mother." It was summer's end, 1972, a time of runaway children.

Pictures of Astrid's mother formed in my mind, changing as I envisioned varying chains of events leading to Astrid's departure. Through all the many changes, however, the face of Astrid's mother remained a face of sorrow. Repeatedly in the next few days, I thought of her. Then I simply forgot.

A few weeks later, I stopped at the high school in search of a student looking for yard work.

"Just today a boy was in," a counselor answered, "but I told him no one comes to us—they go to the State Employment for boys."

"Do you know if he's reliable?"

"I don't know—he's new, a transfer from the city. If you want to meet him, go to the library—that's where he goes when school lets out."

"And his name?"

"Clark something—an easy last name like Smith or Jones. You can't miss him. He's the boy with the beautiful hair."

And that, to be sure, was true. He was sitting at the table nearest the door, so that as I entered he was directly before me, his back toward me, his elbows on the table and both his fists supporting his head. His hair was as glossy as cornsilk and neatly trimmed. It was hair the color of autumn—yellows and gold and burnt orange, all intermingled. Softly, I walked to the far side of the table and stood there, until at last he looked up from his book.

But the poor boy's genes had tricked him. They had given him a face that could only disappoint whoever saw his lovely hair first. His skin was pasty and pimpled, his nose blunt, his gray-blue eyes small and close together. Even then, in that confusing moment, I knew, too late, that he had been able to see my response.

He followed me out, and we made some arrangements regarding the work. Throughout our talk he never smiled, and when we said good-bye, I thought of Astrid's mother. Weeks were to pass before I thought of the two of them once again and understood why.

On Saturday at one o'clock, he came to work. At three, I went to the sliding doors between the family room and patio, watched him through the glass and asked him in for cookies and milk. He hesitated and, as he did, his eyes went slowly across the book-filled shelves. When he looked at me again, he thanked me and refused.

At five he stopped, and I looked around in the yard.

"It's very nice," I said. "Would you like to come here every week?"

He said he would, and at one the following Saturday I found him already at work. He had remembered my priorities, and it was clear he would not require supervision. Again at three I went out.

"What would you like?" I asked. "A coke? Something else?"

And again he refused.

"Clark, if you were working at a store you'd get a coffeebreak by now. Surely you'd like one with work like this."

Without looking up from the rake, he said, "I get enough to eat," but he had emphasized, however slightly, the word "eat," so that the inevitable next question was, What don't you get enough of? I hesitated, but then I asked.

Steadily moving the rake, he said, "I need a place to stay."

I was sorry at once that I had ever gotten involved with him, and because of that, and because I had no intention of taking him in, I find it hard to explain why I asked any more.

"Where do you stay now?"

"I have a room on Bryant."

"With your parents?"

"No."

"With relatives?"

"No." Then, abruptly, he stopped raking and fixed me in place with his eyes. "I pay for it," he said—firmly, but without hostility. "I work every night, six nights, busing tables. I make good money, and I always pay my way."

He waited for my answer, holding me there with his solemn eyes.

I lied. "I have something on the stove," I said.

At five o'clock, I said, "No one's ever done the yard so well in so short a time, so I'm paying you eight rather than six. But as for the other thing . . . ." He was concentrating on my words, squinting from the effort, so that his eyes seemed even smaller, and creases formed between them. He knew what I planned to say.

"But can I come back next week?" he asked.

"Well yes, I guess so," I said. "That was what I agreed to." As he turned to go, however, I added, "If for some reason I want to get in touch with you, like if I didn't need you—just one Saturday, I mean—how could I reach you?"

The creases reappeared between his eyes. I was sure he had guessed I planned to send a note with some polite excuse that ended his employment. Slowly, he shrugged. It was a gesture of utter despair.

"Phone the school," he said. "They take messages."

I felt ashamed to my very core.

All week I wished that Clark would never come again— that he would not even tell me, but rather just stand me up. I had begun to feel responsible for him and wished he would set me free. I could tell no one about his request, however, afraid that my husband would have fewer qualms and send the message. That would have added to my incipient guilt, and needlessly, I felt, because I hoped I'd still be able to solve the problem, somehow, without becoming involved. When my husband, therefore, seeing the well-groomed yard, remarked that this boy I'd hired was a winner, and my son scowled at the insult to himself implied in any praise of any other young man, I merely said, "He doesn't work like a boy at all."

The boy came again, as I had feared he would. I was

waiting for him where we keep the garden tools.

"I want to talk to you," I said gently.

"I really want to work here," he said, "and I won't talk about living here, never again."

Some moments went by, and I asked, "How old are you?"

"Seventeen."

"Why did you leave home?"

"My mother's new husband says he wanted a woman but not her kid besides. My father has a different wife too. He says I'm old enough to shift for myself—why do I bother *him?*"

"Why did you come down *here?*"

"Because I heard your school is good. It's harder, but maybe here I'll get to be an educated man."

That last phrase was too much for me. I asked him to start and promised we would talk a little later. I went indoors to try to analyze why I was feeling so pained. It was that phrase: "an educated man."

I myself had two sons, and I was sure I had never heard either one of them use those three words together. The phrase was archaic, or perhaps the very aspiration was archaic and alien to the world of the seventeen-year-olds I knew. Clark himself seem archaic, and again I remembered and this time understood why he had reminded me of Astrid's mother. His eyes were sorrowing, as hers must be. He seemed old, experienced, buffeted—not of Astrid's generation, but of her mother's and therefore of mine. He spoke in tones that set up resonances deep inside of me from feelings I had forgotten were there. To aspire to be an educated man—it was something I could understand.

I poured a glassfull of milk, cut a slab of pound cake, and carried them out to the patio table. Clark was rolling the mower across the patio onto the grass.

"Sit down," I said familiarly—and somewhat sharply too—"and drink that milk."

He stopped and, still holding the mower, stared—long enough for me to see that the sharpness with which I had spoken we normally save for those we love.

He let go of the mower and, his eyes still on mine, slowly sat down at the table. His nostrils widened, and I was afraid that tears would come next, but they didn't. Instead he turned, lifted the glass and brought it close to his lips. His hand began to tremble, however, and a rivulet of milk tumbled over the rim and down its side. He kept his eyes on the glass, and his jaw hardened, perhaps from the effort to steady his hand, and still he couldn't bring himself to drink.

"Oh, Clark," I said, "I'm sorry. I wanted you to be young." It was clear he didn't understand. "Don't drink it," I said. "I mean do, if you want it, but not if you don't. Or leave it for later—whatever you want."

I turned and hurried indoors, and all afternoon I didn't look out. I had upset us both, but we never referred to the moment again.

At five I went out and paid him.

"Clark, the room you have on Bryant—what's wrong with it?"

"You read books," he said. "My landlady's an old woman and doesn't know much. When I get stuck on some homework, there's nobody there to help me out."

The relief I felt was swift and intense. "Is that all? Down here you get help from the teachers. Tell me whom you have." He was shaking his head. "I do that for my own son. I'll get Mr. Cohen for math and Mrs. Turner for

English. They'll help you after school—they *do* that—you won't have to move."

"No," he said, "I don't belong down here. The principal will think I'm being a bother to him and make me get out."

"No, we don't go to him. A counselor can do it."

"No," he said, "I don't want to bother anyone." He paused. "But Saturdays—can I still come back?"

"Of course," I said.

He mounted his bike and, chin down, rode away in the autumn dusk under the elms, which were the colors of his hair.

I returned to the patio table. The cake and milk were there, but the side of the glass had been dried, and the table was clean. He had set the cake plate over the glass and inverted the saucer over the cake, so that both cake and milk would be protected from dust and remain of use.

On Monday, I phoned the counselor and asked that she send him a message to come to my house on Wednesday, if he could, to do a little job, but he didn't appear till Saturday noon.

Without greeting, he said, "I can never come on weekdays. I have to do my homework first and then go straight to work."

"When do you have your dinner?" I asked.

"At the restaurant. It's part of my pay."

"Do you need this yard-work money for your rent?"

"No," he said. "It's for a luxury."

I smiled. "Would you tell me what luxury?"

Simply, with no malice, but with no apology either, he answered, "No."

That evening, I asked my husband if Clark might live with us. He was incredulous. "Tom's room is vacant anyway," I added, "and the boy would pay for it."

"Who wants his money?" he said. "Aside from having a stranger wrecking our privacy—a boy you don't even know? Don't we have problems enough with our own? Who wants *him?*"

"No one," I said. "That's the point." I told him everything I knew of Clark and pointed out we'd seldom even see the boy since he worked in the evening. He heard me out and then refused.

I could see the conflict my husband faced. I was sure that what this dull archaic boy had done to me he must have done to him as well. I knew my husband was comparing—bitterly—Clark, seventeen and striving toward his manhood, with our older son, twenty-one, shacked up in Berkeley and making candles. Or with Dave, the younger one, eighteen, lazy and sullen. We didn't say anything more about Clark for the rest of the week.

The Saturday after, however, my husband returned from his office in mid-afternoon. It was something he rarely did, and even then he would phone in advance.

"Is something wrong?" I asked.

"No," he answered, "I just wanted to see that boy."

He didn't go out to meet him, however, but sat in a chair in the bedroom, watching from the window, brooding. It made me uneasy. I was afraid the boy would notice him and reproach us both, if not in words, through his eyes. I went outside, rearranged some chairs and looked toward the room. From the sunlit outdoors the room looked dark, and my husband couldn't be seen.

In a little while, he joined me in the kitchen. "In addition to everything else," he said, "Dave would be jealous."

"I'd bend over backward to prevent it. Besides, Dave

doesn't get home till dinner. That girl he spends his afternoons with. . . ."

My husband waved his hand, cutting me off. He didn't want to be reminded of the friends his son was keeping, and least of all of the girl. He went to the family room and watched for a while from there, where Clark could see him. Then, suddenly, he opened the door. "Clark!" he said. "Get *in* here!"

I was appalled by my husband's tone, but I could see Clark clearly, and I know he wasn't cowed. If anything, he stood even taller now than before. With no haste at all, he set the pruning shears down on the table, slapped the legs of his jeans and scraped the dirt from his shoes. Deliberately, he met my husband's stare and passed in front of him into the room. Half way in he stopped and looked around as the door was rolling shut.

"Sit down," my husband ordered. "Do you still want to live here?"

"Yes," he answered—instantly, as if he had known all along that the offer was coming.

"Then give it to me from the top. If I said yes, what could we expect of you?"

"For my room now I pay the lady twelve doll. . . ."

"No," my husband said, "I'm not talking about money. When would you be here and what would you do?"

"I get up at seven. I go to school till three. I'd come back here to do my homework. I go to work at five, and I get off at ten, ten-thirty, and I come right home. Saturday morning I do my laundry and clean my room. Saturday afternoon I work in the yard. Saturday night, in the restaurant. Sunday is my day off, and I always go out."

"Do you have a girl friend?" my husband asked. For the

first time, Clark balked. "Well *do* you?" my husband demanded.

The boy's face became belligerent. "I sure as hell do."

"Good!" my husband said. "You're entitled to it."

Suddenly Clark smiled. In all the previous weeks, despite the kindness I had tried to show, he had never smiled.

My husband was at him again. "You spend two hours a day on homework. How can you improve at school on two lousy hours?"

Clark laughed, suddenly, loudly, as though a child could answer *that* one. "Two hours in the afternoons. I finish up at night. Or Saturday morning or Sunday night. Hell, you don't think I could stay in *this* here school on just two hours."

"You had *better* finish," my husband said. He rose, told us he'd leave the terms of our contract entirely to me and left for his office.

I, in turn, left those terms to Clark. He knew to the dollar it seemed, the rents for rooms in different parts of town, in homes of different quality and vintage. He told me what the unused room was worth, and he made it clear that he was paying more for it than for his room on Bryant. It was, however, worth it, he said, because he had "improved" himself.

That phrase, and that quarter hour, marked the turning-point in how I perceived him. A new alert expression had entered his eyes, and I began to see him as self-assertive and strong.

He would not, for instance, agree to let me prepare any breakfast for him, or even agree to cook his own. Kitchen privileges, he informed me, cost extra, and he couldn't afford to pay for them yet. He did, however, expect a little storage space in my refrigerator, believing it something I should be willing to yield, in view of how high was the rent I was paid. With the food he kept there, he assured me, he'd assemble his breakfast and lunch without even touching the stove.

We next discussed the washer and dryer, which he would use on Saturday mornings while he cleaned his room. He intended to pay me the laundromat price, which was thirty cents a load, and when I said I couldn't take his money for a thing like that, he told me, patiently, that in a store the markup is always a hundred percent. "So it has to cost them fifteen cents," he said, and he would compromise at that, take it or leave it. I took it.

As he rose to resume his work in the yard, he said, "Can I move in tomorrow?"

"Why yes, I suppose so," I said. As he turned, I added, "Clark, wait. My husband spoke to you roughly before. Were you offended?"

For a moment he stared. "He didn't speak roughly," he said. Then he added, "But even if he did, when I get you to help me, I'll have my reward."

He went back to his work, and I sat a long time, watching him, wondering why I had done this. I had become afraid. This was not the boy I had meant to help. I didn't know now whether I liked him or not, and I didn't know whether he had changed, or whether I had simply misjudged him before. I, however, had put us on this path, and I could see no way of turning back.

At ten on Sunday morning, Clark arrived, his meager possessions attached to his bike. He went directly to his room,

closed the door and spent the morning alone. I was appre-
hensive, but my husband appeared to be calm, and I couldn't
admit I perhaps had made a mistake. At one, Clark show-
ered, spent a long time in the bathroom, and left.

I opened the door to his room and looked in. Everything
there was perfectly neat. He had left his towel to dry on
the chair at the desk but had shielded the chair with a plastic sheet. In the bathroom he'd cleaned both the mirror and
tub.

When he arrived that evening, it was late, and he merely
nodded and said good night.

As each day passed, I was feeling more assured. Mornings, he'd be out of the kitchen before I was in it, and before
my son was awake. He never left even a crumb on the
kitchen counter, so on Friday morning, as he was leaving
for school, I said, "Clark, I want you to know you're no
trouble at all. You keep the house clean, and the bathroom, in fact, cleaner than the way you find it."

"It's your house," he answered.

In those few words, he had defined our relations. Clark
had established that relationship through an exchange of
goods and services of equal value—as he himself had
assessed their value. As we worked on his homework
assignments that week, I wondered whether he had—indeed
was capable of—relationships based on anything else. He
gave no clues. I wondered also why he would accept my
time without repayment. It was the single flaw in his carefully structured plan.

My question was answered on Saturday morning. I
returned from some shopping and found he was washing
the windows.

"We didn't talk about windows," I said, wondering

whether he'd know I was trying to tease. "Do you charge the same for windows as for yard work?"

Without even looking at me, he said, "No charge for tutoring, no charge for windows."

In the following weeks, Clark took over the hard janitorial work that I had normally done and much that I had always left undone. He simply would not accept my gift. But this didn't undermine the pleasure I took in teaching him, and pleasure it was almost from the start. Clark was so poorly educated that he couldn't write a paragraph with anything but simple sentences. I felt inhibited at first, afraid of hurting him with constant criticism, but soon I could see he didn't get hurt. He saw his ignorance as no reflection on himself, but as a temporary state that he would overcome, and quickly at that, now that I was helping him. He believed without reservation in my superior knowledge, and though his progress was slower than he deserved, he cherished it.

At the end of the second week, I asked if he felt he had made significant gains.

"I always do," he answered. "I been learning all my life. I can do janitorial work, yard work, and bus and wait tables. But this!" he said emphatically, tapping his notebook, "this especially, this is knowledge, this I have to learn, because knowledge is power."

I almost laughed. "And when you have this power," I said, "what will you do with it?"

"Protect myself," he said.

I thought a great deal about that in the following days. It was not, after all, the most depressing thing he might have said, but it raised again the question I had asked myself a hundred times: What had they done to this child?

He had told me nothing whatever about his past, and on the one occasion when I took a cue from his assignment and asked about his family, he said we didn't have time to discuss it.

Once, however, in a moment of rare intimacy, flushed with pleasure at grasping a concept in grammar, he confided that he kept a diary. Expressing himself in writing was hard, so the diary, he said, had always been more "like lists."

"For instance," he said, "I had codes. Like TINU meant 'things I now understand,'—T,I,N,U, see? And when I'd find out something that I never knew before, I'd write it in the TINU list."

"You mean like now, when you learned something new in grammar?"

"No, when I learned something about. . . ."

I thought he was groping for a word to label his discoveries "About what?" I urged. "People? Relationships? Consequences?"

His expression changed, as though he knew he had revealed too much. "Forget it," he said.

"Clark, diaries are good, but they're not a substitute for people. Do you have any friends?"

"Yes," he said, "I told you right away I have a girl, remember? Please, soon I have to go to work."

One thing, however, encouraged me: Clark had begun to imitate my husband. He didn't see my husband often and, when he did, it wasn't for long, but he was alert to his every movement and word. The expression "in my judgment" was one that my husband had started to use in the Kennedy days, and after hearing my husband, Clark was saying it too. My husband also had a minor facial tic, and before very long, Clark was affecting his tic. It was an imperfect rendition, but it gave my husband something that his sons had been withholding now for years.

I tried to use this fact to Clark's advantage. I proposed that my husband spend some time on weekends tutoring him in math—the only area in which I couldn't help. More than that, though I didn't say it, I wanted my husband to be Clark's friend. My husband thought for a moment or two about my suggestion, but refused. He said he felt we were already much too much involved.

The following day I went to the school to see Mr. Cohen. I told him that a student, Clark Smith, was living with us, and that he needed extra help with math but wouldn't approach a teacher. I asked if he'd consider coaching me as he did the poorer students so that I, in turn, could do the same for Clark, and in a gesture far more typical of Clark than of myself, I offered a fee.

"Don't be silly," he said. "come during lunch—like the kids. Just as I have time for them, I'll have time for you."

During lunch hour the next two weeks, I learned how to use the text, and soon I was helping with math.

Then, one afternoon, Mr. Cohen phoned. "I'm calling to confess. I was proctoring and met him. I said, 'So *you're* Clark Smith.' He got terribly pale. He said, 'Who told you about me?' And all I could think to say was the truth."

"And then?"

"He insisted I tell him how many hours I'd worked with you—exactly how many. And how much you'd paid me. And when I said you hadn't, he said *he* would pay me."

"I'm sorry. I should have told you more about him. He's a good, hard-working boy, but this principle of his—I think it's sick."

"Well," he said, "sick's too strong a word, I think. Don't you? He's a little too serious maybe, but on the whole I find him a welcome change. What I said was, 'Look, Clark, don't make a federal case out of it. I gave Mrs. Kaye a few hours of my time, because I wanted to help her out. *She* gave a few hours of *her* time because she wanted to help *you* out. Now, whenever the time is appropriate, and you find someone who needs a few hours of *your* time, you'll help *him* out, and that's how you pay it back.'"

"What did he say?"

"Nothing. He just stood there trying to understand, and I think he did. In any case, now you know what happened."

And if I hadn't known from Mr. Cohen's call precisely what had happened, I'd still have known it was something important. Clark came home at the usual time but avoided my eyes. "I can't do homework today," he said, and before I could think of an answer, he quickly walked to his room.

Soon he came out and said "I'd like to lay down on the lawn. Do you mind?"

"Of course not," I said.

He went out through the family room, crossed the patio and lowered himself, face down, to the grass. He had most likely never touched that grass except to mow, edge, rake, feed and water it, and now he was caressing it. I turned away.

I hadn't made any plans for these hours except for working with him, and now, without him, I sat at the kitchen table, searching my memory for some clue to what would happen as a consequence of his exchange with Mr. Cohen.

But there wasn't any clue. He had never given a sign of friendship or trust, and he had never given a hint of what he would do if I ever acted against his wishes—as I obviously had.

Shortly before five, I tiptoed out. He was immobile, his face directed away from the house. I walked around him and found him asleep, his face dusty and streaked with tears. I kneeled down and softly called his name.

"You fell asleep," I said when he'd sat upright. "It's almost five."

He needed a moment to gather his thoughts. Then he stood up, and without a word went indoors. Minutes later he left.

When he got back from school the following day, he said, "I don't want to do any homework. There are things I have to think about."

He took his books to his room and then went out on the patio, now without having asked my permission. He removed the cover from the chaise and sat down. As he did, he glanced toward me, and at five, as always, he left.

That night, something woke me, and I went to check. The house was quiet, but from Clark's room some light was visible below the door. I assumed I had heard some noise from there and returned to bed, but I couldn't sleep. All kinds of things were occurring to me. I thought of Clark in tears, disillusioned by what he perceived as my having betrayed him. I heard a sound, as of a chair, briefly scraping the floor, and I pictured him hanging himself. I ran the length of the hall, but then, instead of plunging in, I stopped and tapped at the door. I again heard the scrape of the chair, and then his footsteps, and when he edged the door ajar, I grabbed the doorjamb to steady myself.

"What's the matter?" he whispered. "You drunk?"

"No, I stood up too fast. I saw your light and thought you might be sick."

I returned to bed and fell asleep, and in the morning I woke too late to see him before he left. I went, however, to check on a sinister thought I had had during the night—that he had defaced the room or something in it. I was grateful to see he had not, and I tried in vain to explain away what I had to admit was distrust.

That day, when Clark returned from school, he came directly to the kitchen table with his books, as he had done before he had met Mr. Cohen.

Handing me a sheaf of paper, he said, "I did an extra-credit assignment for English. A story. I wrote it last night."

I riffled through the pages. "In one night?" I asked. "How could you do all this in one night?"

"I did it in one night," he said.

It was a story titled "Duncan and Zazu."

"Oh, a humorous story," I said. He shook his head. "The name Zazu," I explained. "The only Zazu I ever heard of was an old-time movie comedienne. Is it about her?"

"No. But I know who she was."

"Using her name suggests a funny story."

Impatiently, he said, "But her name really was Zazu."

A flicker of intuition came alive in me. "Was his name really Duncan?"

"No," he said, "but it was a handsome name."

"And was he himself handsome?"

"He was when he was little."

"And Zazu—was she pretty?"

"Why don't you just read the story?" he asked.

And so I did. From the first paragraph I knew it was

indeed Clark's writing, and his most recent writing at that. There were many errors, but the compound sentences were of a subtlety of which he'd been incapable just weeks before. For me the manuscript was easier to read than for someone unfamiliar with his style, and I read the pages quickly.

It was a story of two children, a brother and sister. The boy was three years older, though their ages were never made clear. Nor was it clear how long a time the story covered. Only the incidents were clear—the whole succession of them. They held me so completely that the criteria by which I had always judged his papers left my mind.

The incidents dealt with Zazu. Duncan appeared when he was involved—or when a reference to him was of help in describing the girl. I discovered that Duncan knew how to clean toilets, and Zazu did not. Duncan learned fast and remembered, and Zazu did not. Duncan was wary of danger, and Zazu was not. Nor did Duncan feel any need to protect her. It appeared he did not. He merely observed what befell Zazu, and he learned.

And what, precisely, befell Zazu is more than I can repeat. It is enough that I remember. It is enough that Ivan Karamazov memorialized for all time children victimized by their parents. I will let his words suffice for Zazu as well and say only that the neglect, the deprivation, the humiliation, the abuse and the torture of Zazu ended when the child was flung from a window. And still—despite what I have said—I must repeat Clark's own final words: ". . . till one day Zazu was thrown to death from the fourth floor window. And she is buried."

I covered my eyes and wept. Clark said nothing, and I will surely never know what he did during those minutes when I understood at last what they had done to him.

When I had stopped crying, he said, "But I'm sure there's a lot of mistakes."

I took the pencil and started to read. Only then did I see a problem I had never had before.

"I'll show you the punctuation and spelling," I said, my voice cracking, "but that's all."

"But why?" he said. "What about the other mistakes?"

What I had to explain was that I could touch nothing else. I had to tell him that the brokenness of the language was like the brokenness of the lives it described—that he, Clark, writing for once without inhibition, had poured out in one night a volume of words that on any other subject would have taken him a week to write, words that were inevitable and unalterable.

"Did you ever read Huckleberry Finn?" I asked.

He shook his head. I went to the bookshelves and quickly came back with the book.

"Here," I said. "This is for you to keep. I mean that—I will not let you refuse me. Read it, and you'll see what I mean. The way these people spoke, that's the way Mark Twain wrote it down, even though he knew the right words to say and how to pronounce and spell them. Now, in your story, all of it is written that way. What I mean is, there are mistakes, yes, but they're appropriate to the circumstances."

He was shaking his head. "I'll get points taken off," he said. "She expects good English, you know that."

I was suddenly tired, and I hadn't made myself clear.

"Why can't you do what you always do?" he pleaded. "You always help me with the words. You give me better words."

"I could no more change your words," I said, "than I

could disturb that child's grave."

He drew back in his chair, staring at me. After a long time he lowered his eyes. Something in his gesture told me that although in one way he didn't understand me at all, in another way he did. He finally did.

"We have to take this risk," I said. "We have to trust that this teacher will see that these words are right for this situation. And if she can't, the worst that can happen is you won't get extra credit."

"All right," he said.

We read the story together, correcting wherever I could, and when we had finished, I said, "How many people know about this?"

"Only you," he said. A moment later he added, "Why did you cry?"

It was the first personal question Clark had ever asked me. He waited for me to answer, and when I didn't, he asked, "Should Duncan have helped Zazu more?"

"How old was Duncan when Zazu died?"

"Seven," he said.

"No," I answered. "You couldn't expect him to. Seven is a little child, and powerless." He sighed. "In your last sentence," I added, "write that in. Where it says 'And she is buried,' write in 'since the time when Duncan was seven.' "

"But see?" he said. "They weren't really so bad to Duncan. He was just always afraid that they *would* be."

"Still," I said, "He was a little boy. You can't ask such strength of a little boy. Please, make sure you write that in. 'And she is buried since Duncan was seven.' "

"Okay," he said, "I'll write it in when I copy it."

Those were the only words I gave him.

He was about to leave the kitchen when, thinking better

of it, he sat down again and, gripping his loose-leaf binder in both his hands, he lowered his eyes and said, "I want to tell you something else."

I sat waiting for what Clark was finding hard to say. Suddenly, in the garage, there was a click, a rumble and a shattering slam of the heavy door, and then the sound of boots with metal taps on heel and toe stamping across the concrete floor. Before I could assimilate the knowledge that my son was home an hour earlier than I'd expected, there he stood before us, tall and bent and white with rage, glaring at Clark, shrieking, "You mother-fuckin' son-of-a-bitch! You two've been balling."

Clark was silent. Then I heard him answer, "Yes."

I can't remember when I stood up, or when Clark did, or how I came to be standing in one part of the room while the boys were in the other, circling the table. I remember only being aware, as I watched them, that my own son had accused me of this and that the boy I had befriended had confirmed his accusation. I heard a click, and all my attention was fixed on the boys. They had stopped moving. Clark was a little to my left, and in my son's hand was a switchblade knife. I was rooted where I stood, and as had happened to me in dreams, I tried to scream but couldn't.

"Every goddamn *Sunday*," my son went on, "It was you!"

Clark answered evenly, "With me she came. With you she never did."

Only then did I understand they had not been referring to me.

"She made you *think* she came," said my son, " 'cause she liked the presents you bring."

Clark was calm. "I pay my way, but I know she came."

My son made a threatening move with his knife, and I shouted, "Put it down!" but neither of them even glanced at me. Each had his eyes on the other as both—silently now—slowly circled the table.

Clark's head flicked to the rack of knives on the counter dividing the kitchen in two, and I knew that when he had gotten around to where he could reach it, he would equalize the odds. The decision had to be mine. Clark lunged the final segment of the circle and, his eyes still on my son, tapped the vertical rack, spilling the knives to within his reach. I moved forward, and in one long sweep of my arm I sent the five knives flying—striking wall, refrigerator, stove—and then clattering, rattling, echoing, trembling in the half of the room where I stood. The boys' eyes followed the knives, and when they looked at me, they saw me as if for the first time, and in some alien world. Their two faces wore the same bewildered look, and the major difference between them now was the knife in my son's hand. In an uncanny instant, both of them gasped as they looked at my arm. I had felt no pain and felt none even then, but when I looked down, my blood was running in a broad insistent stream from the crook of my arm into my hand.

My son averted his eyes and lowered his knife. He walked deliberately and silently past Clark, past me and toward his room. Clark, however, fixed his eyes on mine in a look of reproach, and at last he gathered his books and followed my son. Shortly after, he left, and I assumed he had gone to work.

The girl was Clark's Sunday "luxury"—the reason for his working in our yard. I wondered whether he'd known from the very beginning that he would be sharing the girl with Dave, and if so, what it meant, but I never asked, and I still don't know.

That evening, my husband and I confronted the facts. It was clear that he was feeling equal parts of guilt for what our son had done to Clark and of bitterness for Clark's intrusion upon our lives. Unable to decide what we should do about our son, he solved the problem of dealing with Clark. Clark must go. We must appease him, pay him somehow to his satisfaction—since he knew a price for everything—and then be rid of him. No sooner had he said all this than, putting his hand to his head, he added, "My God, what am I saying?"

We started again. I had told him only what had happened since our son's arrival. I now went backward—to the story of Duncan and Zazu. I said I knew we couldn't keep the boys together, but to pay Clark off—even to suggest it—would be to cheapen every moment we had had and deny that I had given something genuine.

My husband tried to argue, but half-heartedly, and because he was uncertain about the kind of boy Clark was, there was nothing for him to do but worry.

That night I waited up for Clark, alone, because although my husband had offered to wait with me, it was easier alone. Clark arrived at midnight.

"I was worried about you," I said.

"Why?"

"This late, and you alone out there on a bike. Someone might have hurt you."

He shrugged. "Good night."

"Wait," I said. "Sit down. Please."

He remained standing. "I have to move out, don't I?"

"Clark, what he did today was terrible, I know that. But I couldn't let *you* get a knife too. Surely *you* know *that*. And now I can't keep you both here. He's my son, and even though I'm ashamed of what he did, I can't throw him out. I have to do something about him, and I don't know what, but I can't throw him out."

I had seldom been able to read his eyes, and surely not then.

"Good night," he said, and went to his room.

I couldn't sleep. I kept hearing sounds from his room. Perhaps there had always been sounds, I thought, but that night I was hearing them.

Near dawn I fell asleep. I woke to the alarm, unnerved. Unsteadily I walked to, and listened at, Clark's door. I tapped and waited and finally turned the knob.

He was gone. The linens were neatly folded and stacked on the chair. The furniture was freshly polished, the scent strong in the room. In the dresser drawers and closet there was nothing left to show that the room had ever been his.

I phoned the school at nine and was informed he hadn't attended his eight o'clock class. At noon I learned he hadn't been at school all day. Why was I inquiring? they asked. Who *was* I? Fearfully, I scanned the evening papers.

News, however, came the following day, in Clark's writing, in the mail addressed to me. There were diary entries, photocopies, and neither of the pages was a list.

Today S. told Dave she has been balling with me. Dave came home and pulled a switchblade, so I tried to grab a kitchen knife, but Mrs. Kaye stopped me.

She knocked them on the floor and cut her arm, but then I didn't need the knife, because Dave got shook and put down his.

Now she says I have to move. I saw it coming.

3:20 A.M.

It would really not be good to stay here any more. I see that now, even though at first I didn't want to have to go. Dave is not like me, and she could not tell him to go away and shift for himself. He would not be able.

Besides, she does not send away sons. It is really not normal to send away sons. It is a thing I now understand.

4:00 P.M.

(I always write at night, but today I want to xerox this and mail it going to work.)

I have my room on Bryant back. It was empty all this time.

I missed the morning, but I went to school in the afternoon, and during lunch I talked to Mr. Cohen. I told him Dave and I were fighting, so I moved.

I asked if he would help me out with Math, and he said he would be glad to. He also said, "Continue getting help in other subjects too," and I should ask the teachers. So I will.

I also think I better not go back to do the yard work. Besides, I don't need all that extra money now.

Some day though, when I think the time is right,

but not too long from now, I'll send Mrs. Kaye a letter. I'll tell them about the things I'm doing, and then, if she still wants, and she invites me to their house to come and see them, I will be glad to go.

Two Hours
in the Life of
Steven Malinowski

Steven is twelve years old and epileptic. He's been in many hospitals in recent years but never in one like this: its playroom, which is divided in half by a movable screen of vertical slats, has a pool-table—new, perfect and strictly for those who are twelve or more. The cue-sticks and balls are locked in a fabulous closet to which Irene has the keys.

Irene is twice his age, dark-haired and tall, and Steven is sure she loves him. When she sits on his bed, she puts her face up close to his and winks. As he waits in his room, he pictures the plaque on her desk: Recreational Therapist. Irene Lane.

His thoughts shift to his mother. She worries whenever he's all by himself, so he promised if no one his age was admitted today he'd spend some time with the "ladies."

The ladies are volunteers, and he's heard them referred to by nurses and aides as incompetent women who wouldn't get paid for their time, so they give it away. To him, they're nameless, though their names are on their pinafores, and they're old, meaning older than his mother. Here, though they're old, they take orders from Irene, who's not only paid but young. He's amused by this and proud of Irene. His amusement vanishes—remembering the ladies has reminded him of Jess.

Jess is ten months old. In his forehead is something that looks like a paralyzed worm, and over his chest is a dressing that slowly gets yellow and wet. Steven has no idea of what can be wrong but assumes if it happened to Jess it can happen to him. Still, he doesn't intend to disclose his fear to his parents, nor of course to Irene.

He goes to the playroom, enters on the side that has the pool-table, and separates the screen. At a low circular table, little children and a volunteer are making paper butterflies. Nearby is a girl, about nine, blond, sucking a popsicle.

Seated beside them all is a lady and Jess, who is propped up high on a pillow in a small red wagon. The lady smiles that exaggerated smile that adults put on for babies.

"See the boys and girls, you dolly? Some day *you'll* be as big. You will, you good little baby, you will."

In the five days since Steven first saw Jess, only once has he heard him cry. Steven has absorbed without a moment's doubt the judgment that a child who doesn't cry is "good," and he's sure that he himself never was as good as Jess.

Yesterday was when he heard him cry. A doctor and Angie, a nurse, had come to the playroom. The doctor squeezed what is under the skin of the infant's forehead, and Jess cried out. From the doctor's frustration, and from the anguish in his and Angie's faces, Steven surmised that Jess will soon die.

As Steven approaches the wagon, the lady says, "My name is Helen. What's yours?"

He answers, kneels and brushes the baby's legs in a soft caress till Jess is grinning and kicking his feet.

"How gentle you are," Helen says. "Would you like to play cards? We'll talk to Jess as we play."

"Thanks, but all I like is playing pool."

"The things you'll need are all locked up, and the therapist—her name's Irene—doesn't arrive till ten."

He's already bored—all she can say is something he knows. He says he'll wait in his room, and he turns to leave by the door by which he came in, when the blond girl, eyes on him, follows. He hurries to be in position before she can let her popsicle drip on the table, and waits, his arms crossed on his chest till the girl, intimidated, leaves.

"Steve," the woman calls, "and you too, dear"—to the girl—"let's take Jess for a walk in the halls."

She offers the wagon-handle to Steven and asks him with whom he plays pool, since when, and whether he's good at it too. He says, "With my dad, four years," to the first, and in answer to the last he shrugs.

"That means you *are,* and modest to boot. I don't know a thing about it—tell me the rules."

As he starts to explain, the girl bends down to Jess. She tells him she's leaving today but will visit and bring him a toy, but soon she forgets him and edges closer to Steven.

Jess cries out. He has slid from the pillow. His head is bent to a side, and his chin is pushing the yellowing gauze, making it fold. Helen panics. She straightens his head and clutches his legs to keep him in place, but his cries go on.

"I'm afraid to move him up," she says. "This opening here in his chest—what if there's one in his back?" Steven is now caught up in her fear. "Go slow," she tells him, "and I'll hold him like this till we've taken him back."

Jess is crying hard, and their panic grows. When they reach the desk the clerk informs them, "Angie's *somewhere*. The aide's in the lounge."

The blond little girl runs to the door of the lounge, sees who's there, and without having asked for help, hurries away. Steven and Helen go on but, reaching the lounge, they stop.

The aide is slouched on a sofa, her legs up high and wide apart. Ropes of smoke rise from her nose. "Get Angie," she says, "I'm having my break," and Steven—despite his expertise as a patient—is stunned. He'll remember this aide always, but by the time he turns sixteen he'll have heard equivalent words from so many other people in so many other settings, that he'll think of this scene as another cliché. Now, however, when he's twelve, he's stunned.

He turns to Helen just as she turns to him. Her face is flushed, and when he sees in her eyes the progress from shock to rage, her face and her name are fixed in his mind, to be remembered decades afterward with feelings as warm as those for the young and beautiful Angie, who now comes running beside the blond little girl—who at nine is already wise.

Angie lifts the infant up and places him high on the pillow, and Jess is quiet almost at one. Angie kneels. "Oh my poor baby," she says and kisses his face. She assures them it's safe to move him whenever they need to, and Steven is sure he was stupid not to have known this himself.

They're seated on child-size chairs in the playroom, off by themselves. The blond little girl has gone, and Helen is stroking Jess's face. She has not smiled once since she heard him cry. Steven moves his chair until it touches hers.

"Helen? What's that thing in his head, do you know?"

"A tube. He gets deposits of fluid in his brain, so they put in a shunt to carry the fluid away. I should have known: one tube, one opening. I could have moved him myself."

"Could the same thing happen to me?"

"Oh no, Steve, no, it's not connected with your condition at all." She moves his hair away from his eyes. "It's an illness you just don't have—you'd know if you did."

He breathes a sigh and knows he's revealed much more than he planned, but he's glad.

"Does it ever work?" he asks.

"The shunt? Of course."

"But not on everyone."

"I don't know about everyone, but look at how chubby and healthy he looks. *He'll* be all right."

He can't tell her that on this she's wrong. He has to get back to his room and think the things that make him feel good.

He's stretched across his bed, picturing Irene. She'll arrive and unlock the closet. She'll check on the children unable to come to the playroom, bring them some toys and then give Helen instructions. But now the image of Helen following orders doesn't look good, so he drops it and goes to another: Irene will get finished with all the details, select a cue for herself and play him a game. "Terrific!" she'll say when he makes a difficult shot, and he will be playing his best. He feels a longing, a yearning so intense that he's afraid that someone's watching from heaven, reading his thoughts. He hides his head in his pillow and waits.

Suddenly she's here—he smells her perfume. "Did you miss me?" she asks. He nods, and she fingers his corduroy robe. "You look terrific in red."

He hesitates and answers, "So do you."

"Tomorrow I'll wear something red. Specially for you."

Before he can say "Your shiny blouse," the blond girl, now in a dress, comes in and embraces Irene, who returns the embrace, and Steven is angry and jealous.

Irene, still holding the girl, says, "You're going home! What did I say the day you arrived?"

"That I'd have the operation and be cured."

"And?"

"And I'm cured!"

Steven stares at the girl as if CURED were stamped on her forehead in gold, and Irene notices and understands. She gently pushes the girl to a side and takes Steven's lapels.

"Don't be jealous, Steve, please. Dr. Price is standing in frogs up to his navel so people like you can be cured."

In later years he'll recall she was sad—she wasn't so sure Dr. Price would succeed—and he'll wonder whether, had they been alone, he'd have told her he loved her. Now, however, she wants him to laugh, but he doesn't find her image of research on frogs funny at all.

She jabs him lightly and stands. "Enough of this jazz. You can be a champion—as good as Paul Newman and Minnesota Fats. Get out to the pool-table, now—up up up."

Though he's not really cheerful, he's cheerful enough, and by the time she gets to the table to play him a game he's all warmed up and playing swiftly, expertly, giving her hardly a chance. The click of the balls replaces the taunts of children who see him get sick, and he feels himself handsome and powerful, full of the strength of this massive and wonderful table, and finally totally free.

He's tired. He stands at the closet returning his cue, and Irene reminds him to go and get ready for lunch. She draws the halves of the screen together between them, and then, with Helen, takes the little ones back to their rooms. He stands alone, unsteady, and decides he should sit for a while.

Irene and Helen come back to the other side of the room.

"Two weeks," Irene says, "mostly at Waikiki."

He presses his face to the screen, thinking he ought to speak up, but he doesn't expect to be caught, so he doesn't.

"The children will miss you," Helen says.

There's a moment's silence. Then Irene answers, "It's the toys and the table in there that they love."

"That's absurd," Helen says. "the children adore you— you know it. But before I forget—who'll have the keys?"

"*I'll* have the keys."

Helen looks puzzled. "I mean the keys to the closets."

"I know. There's enough to play with just with the things I leave on the shelves."

"For the little ones, yes, but the better board games and the pool-cues. . . ."

Helen stops, but Steven understands that patients older than six will have access to nothing they'd normally want.

"But you needn't give them to *us,*" Helen says. "Give them to a nurse. We'll get them from her and return them to her."

"I'm a professional, Helen, remember that. Nurses don't entrust medication to *me,* and *I* don't entrust recreational therapy to *them.*"

"But when nurses go on vacation, other nurses go on in their place."

"Then there ought to be an assistant for *me.*"

Steven is confused. He believes Irene should leave the keys, but he doesn't want her to be upset. In her voice there's a sound of meanness he never has heard there before, and he isn't ready for it and can't understand.

In Helen's voice there's a plea. "But Irene, volunteers mean nothing at all to the children. We come and go, and to them we're alike. It's you they love. We aren't here to compete."

"As if you could!"

Helen seems to shrink, and Irene—ice in her voice—says. "This is not a baby-sitting service. Don't ever forget."

Irene marches from the room. Steven has never seen her get angry before, and it's Helen who caused it. He *hates* Helen. He hates her as much as he hated the aide who hadn't helped her with Jess. He watches her walk to a shelf, remove her purse and leave. He wants to run out to Irene, but he'll have to admit what he did, so he stays in the chair.

Some minutes go by, and Helen comes back through the door near him. "Steve? Why are you still here?" He refuses to answer, and her voice becomes soft in a way that moves him in spite of himself. "I went to your room to say good-bye," she says. He turns his head so as not to have to look at her face. "You heard us quarrel, didn't you?" He doesn't believe he owes her an answer. "It's okay, Steve," she says. "Thank you for helping with Jess. I hope you'll go home before I get back here next week, but if you don't, I'll see you then."

She waits, but he will not give in, and she leaves.

He stands and goes toward his room. The silver wagons carrying lunch are coming along in the halls, rattling, giving off smells of food he doesn't want. He sees the girl who is leaving, cured, and he averts his eyes.

He sits in an armchair, closes his eyes, and again he concentrates hard. It's tomorrow at ten. He will still be alone in the room, and no one at all will come in until it's Irene. "Steve," she'll say, "see what I'm wearing today?" He'll act grown up. "You look pretty in red," he'll say. Her shiny blouse will shimmer in the morning light, and he'll ask, "May I touch it, Irene?" He'll brush his fingers lightly over the sleeve, and he'll say, "When I leave, I'll miss you." And she'll answer, "I'll miss you too."

Preservation

It was Elaine's friend who was calling me. "Anne? Yesterday—guess who I met downtown. Scofield!" I pulled the phone away from my ear. "Hello?" she said, "Hello?" and when I answered she said, "He's panhandling! Elaine's wonderful son."

"You told her you saw him this way?"

"Not yet."

"For God's sake don't! She doesn't want to hear of him."

"That's what she *says.*"

"Then give her credit for knowing her mind."

She hung up, and pictures of Scofield sprang to my mind: a boy of twelve in a musical, bowing to wild applause; at eighteen, promising my daughter Susan love and delivering rejection; at twenty, overdosed on heroin, his breathing at last restored.

I called the woman back. "Did he say where he lives?"

"Cowper at Forest—that's all he said."

I put the leash on the dog. "First an errand," I told him, "and then your run in the park."

It was foggy, more like a morning in summer than spring. We were on Forest, and as we reached Cowper, the dog, by some sense I wish I could name, knew he had never been there and sprang to his feet. I parked at the second house, a building where an oral surgeon had his offices and, through the rear-view mirror, dimly saw an abandoned house.

I left the dog and crossed to the aging homes where I'd heard that the owners rent out rooms. Only then did I begin to wonder which was the house where Scofield lived—and then, bewildered, realized I didn't even know why I had come.

I didn't want to meet him. I'd lived for years afraid he'd return and work himself back into Susan's life, and as I stood there shivering, I sensed I had come to gauge his strength. But Susan wasn't a child any more, and her choice, whatever it was, had to be hers. I turned to cross the deserted street, back to my car, and now, for the first time saw— clearly—in the uneven enveloping fog, the abandoned Victorian house.

I was seized by a chill, and my eyes clamped shut, but I knew I was overreacting and opened my eyes.

The house's façade was dark through the faded paint, the lower half of its door was gone, and windows were broken throughout. I was sure it was teeming with vermin. Slowly, I moved to the porch to examine a notice tacked to the rail.

WARNING. DO NOT ENTER. UNSAFE TO OCCUPY
City of Palo Alto. Department of Engineering.

I turned to my car, but I couldn't leave. I wouldn't allow a vacant house to send me running away.

From the driveway of the surgeon's office, I looked at another side. Behind another warning notice was a bookcase, holding metal cans, as if the house were still in use. Above it was a broken outdoor stairway, dangling free, and in a second-story window frame were ragged sheets of dried-out plastic.

Walking the alley that bordered the yard, I hurried toward Forest. There, stopping, I looked higher, and a thinning fog revealed the topmost story—charred, gutted. From blackened rafters strips of roofing matter hung like flattened men, and in the roof a gaping hole exposed a silver sky. I lowered my eyes. For the first time, I saw there was a basement, and inside, at the edge of a glassless window, something wide, like a bed, and behind it something vertical, irregular, dark.

"Wanna come in?"

I turned and ran, knowing of course who it was, and heard him laugh. I wheeled around. He was now on the bed, coming forward on hands and knees, his face at last protruding out the window frame and grinning, pale and gaunt.

I couldn't reconcile his loud undamaged laughter with his damaged face. At last I found my voice.

"Scofield! Come out of there this instant!"

His second burst of laughter was appropriate. Long ago, when I could speak to Scofield as I spoke to Susan—because he *was* a child, and because he knew that beneath the sharpness of tone there was always affection—then he would not have laughed.

I walked away, hearing his steps on the weeds, and soon, at the corner, he caught up. I turned to the car, and he stayed at my side. Then, with an obvious effort, he skipped ahead and stood in my path. His head was cocked and his lips were parted, showing a space in his upper jaw where a tooth was missing.

"Why won't ya come in?" he said.

"In that ruin?"

"Nothing's gonna happen." I shook my head. "So take me to *your* place." Again I shook my head. "Then where you going?"

Reluctantly, I answered, "Taking my dog to the park."

Surprised, "You have a dog?"

"If you like," I said, "you can come with us to the park."

He brought his hand to his face and tapped his lips with two of his fingers. "Will you bring me back here after?" he asked. I nodded. "What the hell," he said.

He followed me toward the car, and when I opened the door, the dog stood up, his 120 pounds stretching across the top of the bucket seat. Scofield gasped and backed away.

"You're living *there*," I said, "and afraid of a *dog?*

"I'm *not* afraid of a dog. I don't trust Dobermans, and that's what you go and have."

I waited. "Are you getting in?"

"Does he bite?"

"He's never seen the need to before."

Hesitant, Scofield extended an upturned palm as little as pride would allow. The dog sniffed, drew in his head, turned around in the limited circle allowed by the seat and eased himself down. Scofield got in, forward on the seat and looking toward the back.

"His name is Dietrich," I said.

"Dietrich," he repeated—scornfully. "Jesus."

We drove in silence, and Scofield repeatedly, nervously, glanced to the rear. When we reached the cross-street nearest my home, I made the turn and saw him grin. I stopped the car in the driveway, and he, instantly, opened his door.

"I'm going for a thermos," I said. "Wait right here."

"I can't come in?" he asked.

The sudden hurt in his eyes, the sound of loss in his voice—and a sense, undefined, of some loss of my own—came together and shook me, but I didn't change my mind.

"You won't let bygones be bygones?" he asked.

"Which bygones?"

"Bygones!"

"*Which?* You mean you've reformed? My God, *look* at you."

"Who the hell do you think you are? You used to *hug* me."

"I don't *care* any more. That *you* could come to *this.*"

"To *what?*"

"You can wait right here or go back on foot."

"How do you know what I'll do to your car?"

I opened the windows and then my door. "Dietrich is here."

Scofield got out of the car and slammed the door. Dietrich stood up, extended most of his body out of the nearest window and sniffed the air where Scofield stood. I entered the courtyard alone without looking back, and when I returned, Scofield got back in the car, his anger apparently gone.

At the park, the enclosure for dogs was deserted, just as I liked. With other dogs around, Dietrich would socialize rather than run, but alone and the leash removed, he'd run like a beast pursuing his prey. Then he'd stop, sniff, mark his territory, bound across the field again, swerve at the final second avoiding the fence, at every turn increasing his speed, joyous and free. Scofield watched him, entranced.

"Dietrich!" he called.

The dog, poised above a gopher hole, looked up, waiting to hear the command. I could have said, "Say 'Dietrich, come!,' " but I begrudged Scofield even that.

Dietrich returned to his gopher. Scofield slouched against the fence, defeated, and with that single gesture shamed me.

Soon he said, "How come my mother didn't come herself?"

"How could she know where you were?"

"Same way *you* knew. You ladies stick together."

Suddenly—elated—he said, "He's coming!"

The dog was coming, but at a negligent pace, not as he did on command. Scofield went forward to meet him, but Dietrich dodged him and came to my side. From the bag I had brought I removed a bowl, set it down and poured from the thermos.

Scofield, incredulous, asked, "The drink's for the dog? Did you also pack him a picnic lunch?"

"It's clear your *brain* isn't destroyed."

"*Nothing*'s destroyed," he said. "And it's *my* body, *my* brain."

"And nobody else got hurt, right?"

"Look!" he said, in a tone that was more ultimatum than question. "If I pet him, will he bite?"

I wanted to say, "How should *I* know?", but I couldn't. At last I said, "Of course not."

The dog had finished and now was mopping his face with his tongue. Scofield extended his palm, and Dietrich, without hesitation, licked it. Scofield lifted his hand, stroked the glistening jaw lightly, and then with both his hands caressed the dog's head and ears. He knelt and offered the dog his face. Dietrich was quick to oblige him, licking his cheeks, ears, nose, tightly lidded eyes, his closed but laughing lips. Finished, he scampered away to threaten the gophers.

Scofield sat on his heels and watched. His blue and yellow tee shirt, too big for his skinny chest, hung limp.

Soon, from beside me I heard, "Hey, stop it, you. Hey."

He was plucking at his tee shirt, twisting its blue and yellow stripes into undulating swirls. Out on the field where Dietrich stood, blackbirds were circling, squawking, swooping to tap at his rump. Scofield, pointing, fell to his knees.

"It's nothing," I said. "They won't hurt him."

"They will! Stop them! You mothers! You bring him goddamn water, but you let them peck his eyes out!"

Alarmed by his fear, I said, "They don't peck his eyes—it's harmless—nothing comes of it."

"They do! Why don't they *stop?*"

"They have nests to protect—eggs or baby birds—in the trees near the fence." He shook his head. "Before," I said, "they ignored him. Now he's close to the nests, but all they can do is fuss."

Suddenly he understood. He shifted himself to a squatting position and inched himself back to the fence.

But he had said, "You mothers, you bring . . . ," and I

didn't know whether he meant "mothers" literally, or whether he meant the longer word, and meant to refer to parents, or people in general, or those in power, or what. His eyes were fixed on the field, and just as I was about to ask, he laughed.

"He's not getting hurt," he murmured. "He's not."

His tone was one you would use reassuring a child, as if he were all alone, addressing himself. Had I spoken then, I'd have broken the spell. I moved a bit—to see the side of his face—but he didn't appear to notice. His lips were parted, smiling, and he nodded, as if he were back at rehearsals at school. He was bouncing on his heels in a way peculiarly his, a gesture so disarming that they'd used it in the show.

From the field came a bark—enough of you birds!—and the birds flew off. Scofield's joy exploded. His arms went up and out to the sides as he leaned on the fence for support. He made a sound as replete with pleasure and triumph as then, at the end of that innocent play.

"Scofield, why?" I said. "You were so promising then."

He turned abruptly. He stayed on his heels, transfixed, uncomprehending. Then, understanding at last, he nodded, and in the seconds before he answered, his eyes turned cold.

"You know what I was?" he asked. "I was shit."

"You were an actor," I said, "and a standup comic and. . . ."

"*Damn* you." he said. "You're just like *her*."

"Who?"

"Who! My *mother* who. You know how many guys can do the stuff I did?"

"You could have been something else—you didn't have to be a star."

"She wasn't *happy* if I wasn't a star."

He turned, saw the field and lunged for the gate. He was fleeing the dog, who had heard the shouting and come. I fastened the leash and hurried the dog away to the car while Scofield, trembling, pressed his back to the chain-link fence.

When I returned I said, "Don't be afraid—he wouldn't hurt you. Do we stay a while, or should I take you back?"

"To *my* house," he said. "And no more talking! Ya hear?"

He sat in the car ignored by, and ignoring, Dietrich.

"Scofield," I said, "I will not tell your mother I saw you— she told me she's been through enough. So if you want to see her, don't count on me. Call her yourself."

He folded his arms across his chest, and when we reached the house at Cowper and Forest, he entered it just as he'd left it, on hands and knees.

A few days later I was back, but there wasn't any answer when I called his name. I strolled about until an elderly man came out of a nearby house.

"That old Victorian," I said, "do you know who owns it?"

"Cost ya a fortune to fix it up," he said. "Should tear it down—squatters come. Chased 'em—said I'd call the police."

That was in 1976. Scofield did not get in touch with Elaine, nor did I ever tell her I had seen him. But yesterday she said, "Remember the articles all of the newspapers had on the Kennedy boy? The heart infections from needles he shared? I used to think it would happen to Scofield, and I was so angry then, I didn't care. Maybe because it didn't seem real. But now, when it isn't just heart valves but AIDS, now it's suddenly real, and I care. If he had it, I'd stick with him right to the end. There were so many years that were good, and I'd want to save *something* from that." She paused. "But for all I know, he may already be dead."

But Dietrich, we really believe, is the only one who indeed is dead. Even the house at Forest and Cowper is not. Local preservationists were touched by it, and the house, powerless, succumbed to restoration.

Now, in early spring of '87, it is painted the palest beige, and between itself and its perfect lawn there is a row of rhododendrons—as sumptuously white as clouds—and beside them there are red azaleas. There are trees, thriving in our lengthy growing season—spruce and cedar and another conifer whose name I don't recall. And there is also a Meyer lemon tree, young, but pruned to be tall and spreading, rich with fruit whose color, I believe, is like the faded yellow of the stripes of Scofield's shirt.

Marshall in Rome

Often, when his wife is beside him, Marshall has the demeanor of an unsuccessful dog: despondent for having in some way failed or wildly alert for one more chance. It's all expressed in his eyes.

Marge is someone I would call "voluptuous" and Robert would call by some less complimentary word, but we do agree that she's pretty. Marshall refers to her as "Marge," but when he addresses her, her name becomes Ariel. Everyone on the tour appears amused by this, but no one has figured it out or ventured to ask.

I would ask, but Robert warned me that if I elicit one unnecessary word from either one of them he'll pay me back—and I believe him. He took me along on a picnic once with his class, because there's nothing a twelve-year-old likes better than to see his teacher's spouse—especially when the teacher says his spouse is a failed poet but terrific paralegal. When a pupil asked, "What's a paralegal?" Robert answered by waving his eyebrows like Groucho Marx. And when they looked me over and one of the girls said, "What did you first like best about her most?" Robert the educator said, "Her cute little ass."

Our problem during this trip is that Rob—by his own admission—can be very judgmental, and he'd rather be alone than be with fools. I, however, when I'm part of a group, can't bear to separate myself from it for fear they'll label me a snob. Our compromise is that we spend a little time with Marge and Marshall, Robert's eyes signalling me, Bonnie the stooge, when to get ready to split.

As it happens, they and we are the only couples in our early thirties in this group that averages sixty. It was to have been my in-laws' tour, planned-for for forty years, but at almost the last minute Robert's mother had an intuition that if she allowed herself this treat before contracting cancer, the plane would plummet out of the sky. Rather than take whatever refund they'd get, they offered the trip to Robert and me.

Robert accepted on one condition: that I look at the sights and not at the ground. When I was ten, I found a five dollar bill in the street, and I've never recovered. Now I find pennies and, on rare occasions, a dime.

One morning at breakfast, Robert noticed that, as Marge was scanning the room, Marshall was kissing her fingers.

"She didn't sleep," Marshall said. "It's her back."

When I asked about her back, Marge supplied details,

and as I listened, Robert told the others we were saving up our baby-making strength for Rome, so we could give his parents a grandson made in Italia, close to the Holy Father. "Isn't that so?" he asked me sweetly, while everyone giggled or smirked.

I therefore didn't ask, and didn't find out, what's wrong with Marshall's heart, which someone in the group was told is "bad." The fact is, this I really wanted to know, especially after we'd been to Florence, because if his heart is bad, why is he—personally—hauling around her Hartman cosmetics case, Marks and Spencer's woolens, Baccarat vase, Bucherer watches and music-boxes, and Gucci shoes and bags? But if I'd asked, who knows what Robert would have told them next.

Last night, however, Rob admitted that the things he most abhors about them is that Marge has to own at least one of everything made and that Marshall can afford it. Robert! My greening of America lover. His mother's flower-child.

"C'mon, Rob," I said, "worse people than Marshall are rich. Look at what happened last night."

What happened then was that one of our elderly ladies—the wealthiest, I'm sure—was gushing about the Italians. "Aren't they the sweetest people? They're so simple, just like little children—they love two things: their families and food."

Robert, trapped between the woman's condescension and her age, withheld a caustic remark. Marshall, however, said—kindly—"But they really aren't like children, are they? All those beautiful things we've been seeing? Italians made them."

First thing this morning, as I uncover one of my eyeballs, dead ahead are both of Robert's. "One favor," he says. "It's almost the end of the trip, and everybody likes us. I do *not* want my experience of St. Peter's ruined by Marshall and Marge. I do not want to stand under the dome— *Michelangelo's* dome— and hear Marshall say, WOW! Or hear Marge tell me it's a pretty church. Bonnie, do you hear me?"

I still have my morning mouth and yesterday's armpits, and I'm not in any shape to argue. Besides, on this I really agree. I open my other eye and eagerly, like Marshall, I say, "Sure!"

But Someone has had his eye on the sparrow. At breakfast, Marge confesses—sadly—that she and Marshall won't be taking the morning tour. She again hasn't slept, and she'd rather stay and rest, so that in the afternoon, when all of us are at the Vatican Museum and the Sistine Chapel, she and Marshall can shop.

I finally find my tongue and say, "Marshall has to stay with you?"

And Robert, longtime devoted protector of Marshall, says, "Marshall, why don't you take the camera and come along? That way Marge can have some pictures."

Marshall looks at Marge, who says, "Yes, go, Marshall, go, I can manage by myself." Marshall comes along, attaches himself to Rob, and it's not my problem.

But the morning turns serious. We are in the basilica. We have stood at the Pietà and are strolling down the central nave beside our Roman guide. Suddenly music comes on, loudly, and as I turn in amazement to look for the source, Robert points to some speakers and says, "Canned." The music swells and fills the cathedral. It takes control of me, and I don't want to hear another word of commentary from the guide. I don't want to stay with the group. I want to be by myself—to hear the music and feel whatever I feel. I move away from everyone and hurry along the nave. I look up at the dome, which was created by apparent mortals, and try to take it in, not only with my eyes but with some other sense I know is there but cannot name, and something about the dome, something about its dimensions or patterns or blueness, cleaves me in two.

Some German-speaking tourists jostle me, erasing my private world. Robert, though I haven't known it till now, is right at my side. We each have been away a while on a separate silent trip. I take his hand, and he holds mine tight.

I remember the guide and our group, and I want to tell them that we're dropping out and they're to leave without us. I turn to look for them, and that's when I see that Marshall is here, standing on the other side of Rob, and I become aware it wasn't only Robert who was silent, but Marshall as well, and once again I am terribly, almost painfully, moved—just to discover that Marshall was moved.

Marshall? Marshall my soulmate! Robert's twin! Watch it, Bonnie, I tell me, Too much love is unhealthy.

At six, back at our hotel, Marshall and Marge are out in the hall. Marge is trying in vain to open their door, and Marshall can't help—he has designer shopping-bags suspended from every joint.

"Emptied another row of stores?" asks Rob. "When Marge gets finished, Western Europe's gonna look like Poland."

A burst of laughter from Marshall, who finds my smart-alec husband a scream. Not Marge. She does not laugh at what Rob says—ever. She has stopped asking what we've bought, and she reproaches Robert, with her eyes, for my going home from Europe soon with empty hands. Besides, she's concentrating: opening a door is hard. Do women like this still exist?

Robert does not offer to help. I knew that chivalry had died, but I hadn't heard the same was true of good will toward persons. Where is my Robert of the dome? Bonnie, therefore, to the rescue, and I take the key from Marge, which frees up Marge's mouth to say, "And where are *you* two going to dinner?"

I interpret this to mean that *their* arrangements for dinner already are made. "Same place as last night," I answer, as the lock, after the foreplay from Marge, responds to my charm.

Marge, scandalized: "To the same place *twice?*"

Defensively I say, "But it has the best Sicilian food in Rome." What I don't admit is that it also is cheap.

Marshall says, "I've never eaten Sicilian, Bonnie. Ariel? Wanna go?"

Rob wants out. "Marge wouldn't like it," he says. "It's a hole-in-the-wall, and it's cheap, and it doesn't have the ambience that Marge appreciates," and Marge punctuates his sentence with "Then I don't want to go."

Thanks, Robert. Two minutes from now, in our room, I won't even talk. I'll slam the drawers and doors till the whole Visconti Palace Hotel tumbles in ruins. For now though, I say, "I, Robert, not as classy as some, *like* the ambience there. I *like* the big Italian Mama in the kitchen, and I like the waiter, her beautiful son!"

Marshall says, "Ariel honey?" and pyromanic Marge,

excited by the flames that are shooting from my lashes, says, "Aside from pasta, what's Sicilian got?" But the flames are veering from Robert to her, so she adds. *"Okay, okay, we'll go with you."*

Who invited her? Marshall!

But Bonnie the wrecker hasn't slammed the doors at all. I should have. Marshall wanted to go with us, so would it have killed us to give him an evening with*out* going through that jazz? The idiot likes us. And Marge will be busy ingesting and won't even talk. But. Tomorrow's dinner's included. This is our last chance for dinner alone in Rome. In Europe. And we eat early, but Lady Marjorie needs rest before she dines. And she'll dress like Jackie Onassis, so liberated Bonnie has to dress up too.

Robert is solemn. I'm wearing my high heels and my sleek black sheath. He, however, who detests coats and ties, is wearing a sportshirt and Levi's. I go to the bathroom mirror to concoct a fancy face, and when I next look, he has relented without being asked. He's in a pale blue shirt, a dark silk tie and his blazer and slacks. Bonnie, I tell me, Your move! I take from the bureau the picture-books bought in Florence and Rome.

"We still have twenty minutes, Rob," I say. "Want to look at some pictures with me?"

"Okay," he says, and holds out his hand.

The waiter, who saw me last night in flats, pants and my own epidermis, clearly approves of the change, but Robert does not appear to approve of the waiter's approval. Bonnie the consciousness-raiser does, because he's looking at me and not at Marge. When Marge, gawking at the waiter's handsome face, asks if we know his name, Robert says, "Caligula." Robert will get the four of us poisoned tonight, and Marge's sons both will be orphans.

Marge, sweetly, to the waiter: "This first item? Can you tell me the ingredients?"

He, she wasn't aware, doesn't speak English. He turns from her to me and smiles. I smile in response—in spades—and Robert the careful clinician is watching. Through the pupils of his eyes I can see inside his head, where wheels already are spinning.

I am a person who negotiates. "Rob," I offer, *"I'll* stop flirting, if *you'll* stop thinking."

The waiter gets the picture, puts himself back in his place and tells us through his gestures that he isn't rushing us and he'll be back.

Marge lifts her napkin and says, "Eeeuuu." We follow her eyes and discover that the tablecloth is mended, darned by hand, where once there was surely a two-inch hole.

"Maah-arge," I say. "This cloth is ironed, immaculate, starched."

Pedagogue Rob: "In this country, that's the sequence for laundry. First they iron, then they immaculate, then they starch."

Marshall convulses, but Marge is not amused. Nor has she abandoned the menu. She holds it out at arm's length, as if that will help her read Italian.

"So what *is* this?" she asks.

"Caponata? It's eggplant, olives, capers. . . ."

"I *hate* eggplant."

Rob: "Ask for a Mac and a shake."

Blackshirt Bonnie: "Marge! You will *love* the eggplant."

Marshall: "Ariel honey? Put down the menu, doll, okay?

Bonnie's been here before. Let her order for all of us."

Aha! Move over, Robert, *I* have become Marshall's leader. Just act bossy, and people will fall into line. Besides, tonight I can really be boss. They're entirely at my mercy. They speak no Italian—nor do I, but I am Bonnie the brave— and there's no one here to protect them, no quadrilingual tour-guide, no English-speaking Gucci clerk. And who can predict what Italians will do? They shoot knees, don't they?

I'm now in my element, and after consulting with Rob I order for four—pointing to the menu, looking inquiringly up at the waiter, changing my mind when he looks unenthused—and when he leaves, I even feel friendly toward Marge.

"You'll see," I tell her, "there'll be lots that you like."

And of course there is. The pasta is potato-based, and the pizza-bread, the caponata, the Sicilian antipasti, the veal, the eggplant with cheese, the canoli, the zabaglione, the wine—I knew she'd enjoy them. As we walk toward the door, she says, "You know? That was really good!" and the arm she takes is Rob's.

She turns to Marshall. "Where's that store?"

"Ariel," he says, gently, "no."

"Marshall," she says, gently, "yes," but it's a slightly tougher gently.

Robert, who was mellowed by the bellyful of great Sicilian, is instantly alert, and it's obvious why. Marge is coveting another something, and Marshall has told her "no." Marshall's forehead, in fact, is showing some creases.

Marge steps forward, with Robert—as if on a short invisible leash—right at her side. "Let's go this way," she says, and no one rebels.

We're heading west, away from our hotel, and I don't

want to walk this far on heels. I'm about to suggest that she leave just one Italian store intact, but Marge is the sparrow that Someone has his eye on now.

"There!" she says, and crosses the street with us all for a tail. She slips her arm through Robert's again and snuggles close, saying, "Robbie, come and see this darling ring I promise you Bonnie will love, and it's not expensive—you'll see you can afford it."

Robert falters and comes to a halt. Marge Robbies him, tugs him, maneuvers him, surely is going to berth him, and Bonnie the rat deserts the ship. Where, Robert, where are all the wisecracks when we really need them?

I continue to walk—with my head hanging down—because I don't know how to handle this, and I'm not sure why. Marshall is beside me, and though I can't look up at him, I'm sure that he's equally glum, and in this too I'm not sure why. But it's now beginning to dawn on me that, minutes ago, when he told Marge "no," he knew of her plan to get Robert into the store. It was Rob whom he was protecting from Marge, but now I'm angry at him for not being able to stop her, and sorry for him for how he adores her, and angry is bigger than sorry.

I'm really becoming depressed. When Rob and I were together last night—happy—lots of people were out in the street. Tonight, when I could use the comfort of a cheerful face, and so could Marshall, we're trudging along alone. But there on the pavement, in line with pennyfinder Bonnie's shoes, is a chain, and on it a coin. I stop and bend for it, but Marshall beats me to it and has it. Of course! This isn't a nineteen thirties Hollywood movie—this is life.

"The chain is better than the Krugerrand," he says. Robert and a huffy Marge are fast approaching us, and Marshall closes his hand over the find until they arrive. "Look at this," he says. "It was lying out on the sidewalk."

Since it's Marshall's, not mine, I say, "I think we should look for the rightful owner."

Rob says, "How? Put an ad in the paper and interview the multitudes?"

Marge reminds me, "Bonnie, we're *leaving* after tomorrow." She lowers her voice. "Marshall, people are coming. Keep walking, but let me see it," and now "it" is in Marge's hand. She glances down and tells us softly, "Gorgeous herringbone—all it needs is a clasp."

"We're pretty near the restaurant," I say. "Maybe they know who lost it."

Robert, incredulous: "Ask Caligula? You think it belongs to a girl friend of his? It's a tourist who lost it."

"So we can drop it off with the police."

"You think this is Palo Alto? Leave it with some petty bureaucrat, you know who'll get to keep it?"

Marge has forgotten her rage at Rob. "Robert's right," she says. "Why should I give it away? I don't *have* a Krugerrand."

Rob says, "Wait a minute, *Bonnie* found it." He turns to me. "You did, didn't you?"

Poor Robert—he has faith. He can't believe that God would glue my eyes to the ground for twenty years for nothing.

"Rob, we both saw it, and I don't know who saw it first, but Marshall picked it up."

"Okay," says Marge with a shrug, "we split it fifty-fifty. Tomorrow we get the chain appraised, we add the price of the Krugerrand, and Marshall buys you out."

"No," says Rob, "I want it for Bonnie. *I'll* buy *you* out."

Why should they ask Marshall and me? "Rob!" I say. "*I* intend to take her up on it. I don't *want* a Krugerrand."

"I know! Sell it! Get whatever you *do* want."

"Why give a broker a cut?" asks Marge. "Marshall will give you your whole half. Right, Marshall?"

Evenly—suddenly the young Gary Cooper—Marshall says, "Ariel honey, you weren't there and didn't see. *I* didn't find it—Bonnie did. She stopped to look, and all I did was pick it up."

Bonnie *was* there. I *did* see, and even I don't know if Marshall is telling the truth. Who knows who saw it first? But Marge is sure—she too has faith. She isn't looking squinty-eyed at Marshall, the way *I* would be looking at Rob. She quickly hands me the palmful of gold and then, a little embarrassed, tells me she's sorry, she just didn't think. A moment later, she turns again to her husband.

"Marshie," she says, "I want a Krugerrand."

"You want a coin? Sure. Think it over—maybe get a maple leaf. Want another chain?"

"I already have a chain like that—don't you even remember?"

"I forgot for a minute. Want an Amaretto, Rob? Bonnie? Come with us to the bar."

What?

Marshall is here at a table with us, finishing his Amaretto. Marge is at the bar, where English is spoken, arranging to purchase the glasses we've used. She wants to have them and keep them forever, souvenirs of Rob and me, her friends. The waiter retrieves the glasses, and the barkeeper wraps them and gives them to her.

She's back at our table, flushed with pleasure, and handing the package to Marshall she says, "I'll never forget this day, will *you?*" A minute later she asks me, "Bonnie? Want to go to the powder room now?"

"I don't have to."

"Right back," she says.

As she leaves, Marshall turns to watch her, and watches her until she's out of sight. Then he turns toward us again, looking first at Rob and then at me. "Look, guys," he says with assurance, "you don't really know her, you know."

The Kid

He awoke slowly, peacefully, in his own bed in a quiet house, with everyone already gone, while he, after repeated red-eye specials east and late at night returns to the west, stretched languidly and groaned with pleasure. Smoke! At once he was up.

He followed the smell to his son's room and reached the window before there were flames. He blew out the candle, moved it away from the blackened curtain and sat on the bed to steady his legs.

His son seldom came home. He knew that one ought to be glad when a son came home, and he was, but never entirely, even without any incident equal to this. It was simply easier not to be with him—he could forget him awhile. He would have thought forgetting an only child would not be possible, but he had found it was.

It wouldn't be, he felt, if Mark were working at something a father could think of with pride. He admitted there wasn't anything wrong in the choice that his boy had made, but he was disappointed nevertheless. He leaned toward one of the yellow vases neatly arranged on the bureau in rows.

The actual vase-making wasn't the problem. Not so long before, he'd had contempt for all of these youngsters—potters, leathercrafters, jewelry-makers—but now he could admit they'd had a good idea. They were their own bosses. Besides, they often made beautiful things. Right there was the heart of the problem. Mark didn't.

He made only vases and all of them ugly. It sounded funny but wasn't—it was disquieting. Mark acted as if his designs were good, and he, never having discouraged the kid before, was not about to discourage him now. He simply wasn't sure he could judge, except that there had been a moment when he'd caught Mark smiling, a little furtive smile that seemed to say Mark knew his pots were ugly and was glad. But he could not be sure he had read that smile as he should.

He rose and put the vase away. In the typewriter, a sheet of paper arched backward, touching the wall. Beside the typewriter there was a plastic folder, and, opening the folder, he read:

ONE LINE POEMS
by
Mark Marlboro

Marlboro? Like in the cigarette ads?

On the page in the typewriter there was a two-word poem:

FUCK OFF

He steadied himself on the chair. He had had no right to snoop, so maybe, he thought, he deserved what he'd seen. Still, in his own youth, which perhaps had not been rebellious enough to be thought of as normal today, nothing would have made him thrust those words before his parents' eyes.

Without any warning, a familiar unease came slithering over his skin. Bracing himself against a developing dread, he glanced at the floor, under the desk. Then he knelt to see whether something was under the bed. He stood up, opened the closet door and rummaged behind the clothes. Relief swelled in his heart. He started to leave but stopped. He stepped back, moved the door away from the wall, slowly, creating no superfluous current of air, and there it was—a single page ripped from a book, leaning against the wall.

As far as he knew, the problem had started with the high-school graduation. Prior to then, the years since Mark had been born were surely the best of his life. He and his wife had a brilliant and beautiful son who never had given them pain, for whom they had only the highest hopes. But on that disappointing night, when other kids had marched to the platform to loud applause to collect awards, his son had received nothing at all. He assumed that the boy had come in second for everything—he was always among the best—and believed that someone should have seen to it that a kid who comes in second for everything deserves a first in something, even if giving a first requires a bit of finagling.

Later, at home, Mark was reading, cheerful, showing no disappointment at all. He had read his father's mind, however, and said, "It doesn't matter to me what they think. I set my own standards, and if I satisfy myself, it's fine."

"Great," he answered. "No one knows better than I do all the talents you have."

Coldly, Mark responded, "*I* know better." Then, with a sunny smile, he added, "Only kidding, Dad."

As he turned to leave, he noticed a page on the floor. He picked it up and looked at his son.

"I was dropping the book and trying to catch it before it landed, but all I caught was a page."

It was easy enough to believe.

Mark left home for college, and when he returned, he had a gentleman's education but no way to earn a living, so he lived at home awhile, restless.

One day, after making a minor repair in Mark's room, he found, protruding from under the bed, again, a single printed page. He picked it up and knew that tearing the page had been a deliberate act. He scanned the sheet, looking for some explanation in the subject matter, but he couldn't find one. Ashamed for his son, shocked by what, to him, was the uncleanness of having assaulted a book, he felt he couldn't discuss it with Mark. Nor could he tell his wife and discover if she, perhaps, had been finding additional pages.

Instead, he convinced himself that since he knew the many more destructive, and the self-destructive, things that kids were doing, it was foolish to feel such aversion over a book.

Later, before Mark left to share a house with other potters, he found another page, and now another this morning.

In his office shortly after, he lifted the ringing phone.

"Dad? Come and get me, okay? I'm not feeling right."

"How come you left if you weren't feeling right?"

"What difference does *that* make?"

"Look, Mark, I don't work for myself—I can't disappear whenever I want. Take a cab." He waited. "We have to get your car repaired. You can't be counting on mine and then have nothing to use as soon as I'm home." Silence. "Mark?"

"Yes."

"Take a cab."

"I'll be in the library lobby."

"What?" He heard the name of the local college, and then the phone clicked off. "Mark?"

Furious, he rose from his desk. Values should count, he thought, and with values such as his, how did he produce a kid so spoiled? He was taken aback by having this thought. Never before, despite disappointment and anger, had he thought that Mark had been spoiled.

He went to his car and drove away toward the local college. What could Mark be doing there? He had said he'd be at home.

He was sure he hadn't spoiled him. The only doubt he'd had about the way he'd raised his son was a recent question on a somewhat different matter. It had to do with realistic expectations, with what a person could expect of other people, but he hadn't yet explored the idea to its logical end.

When he himself was a child, no one had ever implied that he was entitled to anything special, so whatever the world had given him seemed to be good. But Mark had always been gifted, extraordinary, and it had been right to say so, of that he was sure.

When he reached the college, there was a barricade just inside the campus limits, and before it were two policemen waving the drivers into a U-turn and off. As he reached them he heard, "Only emergency vehicles. Take any road in and around, except for the ones with the 'library' sign."

"But that's where I have to go," he said. "What's wrong?"

"Make your U-turn, please."

"My son's expecting me—he isn't feeling well."

"He'll have to wait. Please move on."

He made the U-turn but pulled the car to the side of the road and parked. Why couldn't they treat him like an equal and say what's going on?

He became increasingly tense. He didn't want to think any more—neither about what he'd done or failed to do in the past, nor about all that was happening now. He remembered some Agatha Christies left in the trunk back of the spare and decided to see if a book would help.

He unlocked and lifted the lid of the trunk, and there below him was a metal cage, a hamster cage, large, filthy, reeking, and in it a pair of hamsters, both of them dead. His other hand shot up. He gripped the trunk lid, held it open a moment longer just to confirm what indeed he had seen. He slammed it down, ran to his seat in the car and locked himself in. He felt he was overreacting but couldn't dislodge the chill from his heart.

Mark had told him he'd bought the hamsters—two females, because he didn't want them mating—and caged them together. Right from the start the hamsters had fought. One was dominant, harrassed the other, kept her from feeding, until the difference in their size became astonishing, and a day arrived when the victim turned and became the aggressor. Whatever she once had endured she now inflicted, and more, with awesome ferocity. Though she still was by far the smaller of the two, she ripped the larger one's coat, drew her blood, tore at her eyes, and finally had her revenge. Mark had said that now there was one.

But there in the trunk were two dead hamsters, and only one encrusted with her dark brown blood. Why hadn't Mark removed her from the cage? And how had the other—the killer hamster—died? Killer hamster? Why should he call a hamster a "killer?" But why not? To God, do humans appear as absurd as "killers" as hamsters appear to him? Is that why the evil go unpunished? Because people are as insignificant to God as hamsters are to him?

He was sweating profusely, and he rolled the window down though he knew his sweat had nothing to do with the air in the car. It was from this onslaught of peculiar thoughts that he never had had before and that, coming upon him now, frightened and bewildered him. He didn't even *believe* in God, surely not in a personal one who punishes and rewards, so why should he now be thinking of God? And how had the second hamster died? Had Mark forgotten where he'd put the cage? Forgotten to *feed* the thing? How could he forget?

Abruptly, he gained control of himself and walked to the officers still at their post rerouting the cars. "The longer I sit there," he said, "the more it seems to me you ought to tell me what the trouble is."

"There's some nut with a handgun up in the library tower."

"He can't hit anything down on the ground from up that high with a handgun."

"You mean he may not hit what he aims at, right?

"Okay, you're right," he said, "but my kid's in the lobby, sick, and I said I'd pick him up. And I won't hold you responsible."

"By the time you get there, the guy could be back in the lobby himself. He picked up a hostage from there."

He started toward the tower, but when he heard "Stop!" he stopped.

"My kid could be the hostage," he said. "Do you know at least who the hostage is? Is it a young boy?"

"All right!" and then more quietly, "All right. I'll find out. Describe your kid."

"He's five eight, good-looking, slim, blond hair, almost brown I mean, shoulder length."

"How old?"

"Twenty-five."

"Jesus Christ! You said a *kid*." The policeman shook his head in disgust, and soon he added, "Go back to your car, will you? I'll let you know."

He waited in the car again, hurt by the cop's contempt and therefore defensive, but conscious of something justified in that contempt, and therefore miserable too. "Jesus Christ!" kept ringing in his ears.

In minutes the cop approached, informed him, "The hostage is an oriental man," and instantly turned to leave.

"Officer," he said, "thanks. I'm sorry. But what kind of a nut would pull a gun and take a hostage here?"

"I don't know," he said. "You asked about the hostage."

Again he waited, calmed by the young policeman's quiet innocuous words. In a little while, he was back.

"It's over," he said. "We still aren't letting the traffic through, but you, you can come there with me."

He was embarrassed. "It's okay," he said, "I can walk."

"Didn't you tell me your son was sick?"

That the officer would take the trouble to bring Mark back to the waiting car was something he hadn't expected, and he thanked him. He went along in the black and white police car, somewhat abashed.

"Was anyone hurt?" he asked.

"No."

"And the guy with the gun?"

"We have him."

They stopped near another patrol car parked at the curb. He climbed the stairs two at a time without looking up, and when he reached the top there were two policemen and, handcuffed between them, the slender young man, unsmiling but, on the surface at least, serene.

When at last he understood whom he was seeing, and sensed that someone else might surely have foreseen this from the moment that he'd reached the campus, he moaned, "Oh, God. My God."

"What God?" Mark asked.

He was startled. He was surprised to hear Mark's voice and puzzled by the question. There was nothing unusual in his having said "My God" but as though there were, Mark was waiting for an answer. From a long-established habit of trying to give a reasonable answer to any question the boy would ask, he searched for some meaning in the inadvertent words.

"Why God?" Mark continued.

His eyes darted to the faces of the two policemen, but unlike his son's, they didn't appear to be mocking. They seemed intent, in fact, on hearing an answer and seemed to be willing to give him whatever time he might need. Groping for what—if anything—his words had meant, he turned from them and back to Mark.

"You don't believe in God," Mark said.

"I know, I know," he said. He was embarrassed before the strangers and confused by what Mark was doing to him. His hand shot forward in a gesture of supplication, and he looked down at it, even further confused, as though it were not his own. When he let his hand drop back to his side, he thought he had gotten a glimpse of an answer. It seemed so unlikely an answer, however, he didn't believe it and couldn't give voice to it then.

Only later, during a prison visit, when Mark looked puzzled by the sudden resumption of a bygone conversation, could he say the answer aloud.

"Maybe without knowing it, I wanted a god. Maybe I needed one. Someone to serve. Someone to love above everyone else. And maybe I took one as people always take gods—on faith, purely on faith."

But now, when Mark is thirty-five and involved in his new life with an older woman and her children, and he no longer comes home, his father believes that that answer in fact was wrong. Submitting oneself to a god, he believes, is an act of deep humility, while his own submission was a form of self-congratulation.

He feels that as he ages he refines his thoughts, and wonders what he will believe when he is truly old—about God, of course, but about other things as well, like whether there is still a place for him in Mark's life, any place at all, and whether he should even expect there to be such a place.

Theresa McCann
and Joe

It happens mostly in fall. The wind comes suddenly—in gusts—selectively stripping the trees, sending a swirl of maroon and orange first from one of the driveways, then from the next, and if droplets of rain should briefly appear, I am twelve years old again, on a tenement stoop in a treeless world, chilled by the wind and intermittent rain, waiting for Joe McCann.

Six steps down to my left is a basement grocery, nobody there but the grocer himself. Nor is anyone out on the street but a girl somewhat older than I, a notorious tomboy—an "unnatural girl," they say, who has spent her childhood on her knees, shooting marbles with boys.

From across the street she calls, "Hey Sara, c'mere. I'll letcha have me a game of stoopball."

Although I'd accept at another time, I don't want to play today. Nor have I in almost a week.

Joe has gone back to work. "He looks good," my father said. "Who would believe he ever took gas?" Earlier he'd said, "I don't understand. A boy with a civil service job, healthy, handsome—why should he not be happy?"

Neither Pete nor Joe has explained. Pete, frantic: "They'll put him in the crazy-house—please don't get any doctor, don't say a word," and my father, to calm him, promised never to tell. He had come upon the scene perhaps a minute ahead of Pete, detected the odor, burst in, wrenched Joe from the oven and earned a secret forever.

My own secret was that I loved Joe. He was twenty-four. He lived with Pete in a flat adjacent to ours—an American-Catholic isle in a sea of immigrant Jews. "We're half-brothers," they said, and so far as I know, no one doubted them, because, though single people normally lived with their parents, it wasn't unheard of for brothers and sisters to live by themselves.

Nor in fact was even a suicide rare. In the four years we lived in that narrow walk-up with its thirty cramped apartments, three tenants had taken their lives—a man by gas and the women by jumping from the roof.

What was more unusual then was that Pete and Joe both were employed. Pete, who was in his early thirties, drove a truck, while Joe was a clerk for the State of New York. He had gone to college, and he read the *New York Times* from cover to cover daily and Sunday.

When questions arose in my brother's homework, or even in mine, which neither of my parents could answer, they would say, "Go next door—Joe will know." I can hear even now my brother's voice repeating for us what he'd learned next door: "Cordell Hull, Harold Ickes, Miss Frances Perkins . . .," and then I hear my father say, "A nice boy—Joe. He must have a good father—the apple doesn't fall far from the tree." "And his mother?" my mother asks. "Also," he concedes.

It didn't occur to me then that, though Pete was almost as old as my father, and though every neighbor addressed every other one formally, not even the children ever called Pete "Mr. O'Neill." I don't know why—whether because he was single, whether it rose from contempt for his being a Gentile, or whether from early on he himself had insisted on "Pete." He was tall, red-haired, good-natured. He played stickball with kids, he allowed us to sit in his truck, and perhaps because, at a time when adults never were carefree, here was a man who was—he seemed like a boy even to me.

Not Joe. He was friendly enough not to be called "stuckup," but not much friendlier than that. There was a sadness, a mystery, in him that evoked romantic ideas. I'd picture myself eighteen, married, my name Sara McCann.

I had learned from Pete that Joe had a sister, Theresa, who taught at a high school nearby. My family never had seen either her or anyone else connected by blood to "the boys," but the evening when Joe nearly had died, the McCanns were all we could think of. Already my father regretted his promise to Pete. What if Joe should try again and succeed? "Their sister," he said, "should be told. She— an educated girl—and the parents too, should know, and they—not Pete—should take care of the boy."

The following evening, my father disclosed that during the day he had phoned Miss McCann. Something was wrong, he was sure. She hadn't sounded upset and hadn't even implied she would come. All she had answered was, "Thank you."

My feelings toward my father now were mixed. He cared about Joe and wanted him to live, but I had heard enough about the "crazy-house" to feel he should not have gone back on his promise to Pete. I snatched my sweater and went downstairs as I often did in the evening, to stand alone in the quiet hallway or out in the dark, deserted street.

I didn't know why Miss McCann had not been upset. I wasn't convinced that I loved my brother much, but I thought that even if Joe had been my brother, I'd still be upset.

From the shelter of the doorway, I saw a woman approach. She paused, peered at the number painted on the house, climbed the stairs and, seeing me only after she'd come to the top and lifted her eyes, stopped, astonished.

She was Joe's perfect counterpart—perhaps his twin. I had never seen a teacher so young, nor one so lovely— slender, with chiseled features and dark blue eyes, with perfect skin and soft dark hair. I turned, went inside and held the door. With leaping heart I said, "Good evening, Miss McCann."

She stared and nodded. "I see," she said. "Good evening."

I hoped she would say something nice about me to Joe.

She walked to the stairs at the end of the hall, and my mind raced. If I stood at their door I might hear, and maybe I'd be of some help to Joe: if anyone came along I'd distract them and chatter loudly enough for Joe to hear me and lower his voice. Quickly, quietly, I followed, listening hard for the door being shut. I took the last of the stairs in silence and stationed myself outside their door, adjacent to ours.

Miss McCann was saying the fault had been Pete's. He had taken a boy too young to know any better—misled him, destroyed him. Now I was sure my father was right in his lack of respect for Pete. Then worse—for me—was the answering venom I heard from Joe. He excoriated her, for cruelty, for blaming Pete, for assuming she knew the meaning of love, for being a part of a merciless mob.

There was silence, and when she finally answered, she spoke to him softly. The family all had loved him, she said— he was their saint. He still could regain what he'd lost if he'd stop, leave Pete, come home, talk to Father Dennis, confess. And then she said some more, including a word I had never encountered: penance.

Joe repeated the word. What he said to her next was peculiar, pompous, as though he were quoting an ancient text. "There can never be forgiveness if there isn't amendment."

She answered, *"Let* there be amendment."

"Please," he begged. "It isn't easy to be what I am. I see myself as *you* see me and hate what I see. I can live as I do or end my life, and either way I'm damned. Yesterday I thought that ending it would be the lesser sin—that it would show how sorry I was. Theresa, while I live I can't change."

"You can," she said. "If you won't, I don't want to hear about you. I never gave your secret away, and *I* don't owe you anything else—tell *that* to that meddlesome Jew."

I entered my own apartment. I sat with the dictionary, reading words here and there, dozens more than I wanted, disguising from my parents my true purpose, finding out the meaning of amendment, penance, damned.

Except for murder, I couldn't conceive of a crime for which you would feel you should forfeit your life. I turned to my father. "Joe's sister was here," I said.

Awed—his awe of teachers was almost equal to mine— "You saw Miss McCann? Tell me, what is she like?"

"She looks like Joe." Then, though I didn't want to give him ideas, I said, "Do you think that Joe and Pete are the kind who would kill?"

"*Anyone* can kill," he said. "In wartime everyone does, but otherwise? Pete who doesn't have a temper? Doesn't even know what serious *means?* Last night—frightened— an hour later he's making jokes. Joe? Something must have happened, bad, so who does he kill? Himself! No. They aren't people who kill."

I was relieved but unwilling to risk asking him more. What I wanted to know was, What else was as bad as killing.

I had a friend named Elaine whom I could depend on to know about terrible things. She lived nearby in a two-flat house that was owned by her parents. On the lower floor were Italian tenants, the mother always in black.

The following day I asked Elaine, "Do you know what penance means?"

"Why don't you look it up?"

"I did, but I don't know what it's for. I thought you might know from talking to Yolanda."

"Why don't you know from talking to Joe?"

"I only ask Joe about homework," I said.

It was clear she knew, and I knew she would tell me— delaying was normal. She had delayed when revealing the facts of "the monthly" and even the scandalous news that the parents of one of our friends were getting divorced.

"All right," she said. "Penance is what Yolanda has to do when she confesses to the priest about herself and Ellis."

Ellis was fifteen, Yolanda fourteen. They were in the same grade as Elaine and I, but they were in the slow class, and we in the fast one. Yolanda was a large and very pleasant girl, and whenever I met her we'd talk. Ellis, who often was with her, was not a talker or even a smiler. He seemed unwholesome, and though I could see why he or anyone else would like Yolanda, I didn't know what she could see in him. But penance for what? This was what I asked Elaine.

Now she revealed the rest—in stupefying detail—what "'sleep with" really meant. Yolanda and Ellis, our parents, Roosevelt, everyone. Then, confession and penance she simply dismissed in a sentence.

For three days I thought about what she had said. All the adults I loved were involved, but only Joe was so ashamed that he alone had taken gas. I agreed that it was disgusting but didn't believe you should take your life. In those three days my concern for Joe overshadowed the rest, and because of this I sat on the stoop that day waiting for him to come home. I was afraid, as my father had been, that he'd try again and succeed. Had I thought he could fool a priest by saying he'd stop, I'd have asked him to do so, but priests, I was sure, were clever, despite Yolanda's apparent success.

When Joe arrived, he said, "It's freezing—aren't you cold?"

I was, but I shook my head and delivered my speech: "I know what you did, but I like you anyway." He stared. "I mean I know what you did *besides* taking the gas."

He sat down beside me but faced forward, watching the

girl with the ball. "What, exactly, do you know?" he asked.

"I heard what you and your sister were saying the other night, and my friend explained it to me. But I didn't tell her who, and I'll *never* tell." He was silent. "Please don't try to kill yourself," I said.

"Don't worry about it," he answered. "If I'm damned, I might as well delay it."

He removed his jacket and passed it to me. It was of a brown wool tweed with flecks of orange, gold and maroon. As I put it on, I glanced at him, but his eyes were still on the girl. She was pitching the ball at the topmost step, then at the one below it, and at the one below that, striking each edge perfectly, so that every time the ball returned in an arc to her hands. Every once in a while she would spit.

"She's Jewish, isn't she?" he asked. "Lucky for her. You Jews don't seem to worry about these things. Or do you?"

I didn't know, of course, what "things" he meant, and I knew no more about what Jew meant than I knew what Christian meant, except that I was one and Joe was the other, but I didn't want him to think me an ignorant child. I therefore thought for a couple of seconds, and then, trying to sound sophisticated, said, "Don't be so sure of that, Joe."

Two weeks later, he and Pete moved away, without having said good-bye.

Before
and After
Celeste

Until I was seventeen, when
Celeste became my friend, my mother approved of whatever I did. If there was something of which she didn't
approve, I stopped doing it, without knowing I had made
a sacrifice. I could have made her happier still if I had given
up books in favor of boys.

My father concerned himself with vital things—war,
political prisoners, the oppression of Labor by Capital—
and the only boys on my father's mind were the Scottsboro
Boys. They, and Gene Debs, Norman Thomas, Mooney
and Billings, were the real America, the present and future
and all that mattered to him as Man, Socialist, Jew. He
never mentioned the word "pogrom"—nor did my mother,
who in all philosophical matters followed his lead—and he
never referred to the Jewish past. He had contempt for synagogues and Zionists, and his hopes, he said, were for all

mankind, but he never felt at ease except with immigrant working-class Jews.

Celeste was two years older than I. She was slim, attractive, self-assured, and were it not for the war and the absence of men, she'd have been what we treasured most: popular.

It was in '42, and we were college sophomores, living at home in Brooklyn. She approached me one day at the end of a French class. "The Richelieu's in port. Do you want to meet some *pompons rouges?*"

"Me?"

"You're the only one I know who's great at French."

French sailors? I could picture my parents reacting to that. I made some excuse.

"Then come to my house on Sunday," she said. "I have French records."

On Sunday, she said, "There's no one at school except 4Fs, so why not *pompons rouges?*"

"I couldn't."

"They won't drag you into bed against your will."

"I know that."

"Your *parents* would object."

"Don't yours?"

"My mother's American-born. You'll meet her. And Leon."

"Your brother?"

"Her lover. But what's the problem. That they're French sailors, or that they're not Jewish?"

"Either would be enough."

I didn't examine our brief exchange—neither Celeste's distinction, casual and clear, between foreign- and American-born, nor my simple consent to an old taboo.

"I feel sorry for you," she said. "Tell me if you change your mind."

I didn't change my mind, but our friendship grew. One day, as I sat at the kitchen table, reading, she phoned. There was a boy named Christophe. He was on a Giraudist merchant-ship that was in for repairs. I listened, and I watched my mother stirring the laundry.

She used to wash the towels and sheets in the bathtub and transfer them, dripping, to a tub she'd lug from the bath to the kitchen and lift to the stove to boil. I can't even guess the weight of that tub, but I took it for granted that that was her work, and she, I'm sure, envisioned the same for me, in time, when—with luck—I would marry.

"I could swear he said 'Jean-Christophe,' but the others call him 'Christophe.' "

I was in love with this boy at once. To me he was Romain Rolland's Jean-Christophe. My mother's hands, on the tub and the wooden paddle, were red and chapped and all but bleeding.

"Jean-Christophe Lacassagne. He's twenty-one. Blue eyes, brown hair, good build. He's a baker."

It didn't matter that he was a baker. You couldn't expect them to need composers on ships, and a baker was fine. Even my father would have to admit it—a baker was "Labor."

"He has friends," she said, "and they don't wear uniforms—they're merchant marine. No one will know they're French or wonder whether they're Jews. Think it over and tell me in class."

It was a painful decision, implying deception, the first of its kind I had made. Nor did I inform my parents until

Saturday noon, when Celeste, according to plan, phoned.

"I have a date tonight," I said.

My parents were both surprised, and my mother was visibly pleased. My father asked, "Who *is* he? this boy."

"A friend of a friend of Celeste. Celeste got dates for Esther and me, and we'll meet in New York."

"I never met her, this Celeste," he said. "What's her last name?"

"Cutler."

"I know a Cutler, a cutter, who once led a strike."

I had to change the subject before I divulged too much. They would not have held it against Celeste that her parents had been divorced, but even my Socialist father could not have forgiven her mother for Leon, and if ever my parents should meet her, either alone or with him, they'd show their distaste.

"Celeste is a Yipsl," I said. It was true, and since the Yipsls were the young Socialists, and Celeste therefore "serious," even my father was pleased, and the questioning stopped.

Christophe, I could see, deserved Celeste. He was handsomer than I had expected, articulate but quiet, and he was clearly the dominant man in the group. Celeste introduced him to Esther and me, and he disposed of us. He gave Esther, who was short, to a boy who was almost as short as she, and me to Henri, who was no more attractive than I. Henri, in fact, looked about twelve, but I had enough faith in Giraud to believe Henri was at least my age.

We sat at a table for six in a little French restaurant.

Neither Esther nor I could release our French, and none of the boys knew English. It didn't matter, though, because Celeste had captured our attention. She calmly discarded most of the grammar she knew, and her accent, which was passable in class when she was reading, was now deplorable in speaking, as she lost her concern for sound in the search of words. Yet nothing could stop her speech nor dim the light that danced in her eyes. She invented words, and those she knew but couldn't recall she replaced with gestures—head held high, like an English princess, she galloped while sitting in her chair. I didn't for a moment begrudge her Christophe.

I saw in her a quality that puzzled me, enchanted me, that only later in life could I name and identify as a human option—an openness to joy. She was a Yipsl, but she wasn't what my father envisioned, serious in the way that *he* meant serious. To everyone who mattered in my world, serious meant seeing life's hardships and not forgetting them, and though they thought they were in favor of happiness, they didn't know how to vote for it. Nor did I.

When I got home that night, my parents were waiting up. They neglected to ask whether I had enjoyed the evening.

"He asked you for another date?" my mother said.

"Yes. Tomorrow evening."

"Good."

"Not a separate date. All six of us."

"That's perfectly all right," my mother assured me. She held to the momentum theory of popularity: if you had a date, someone who knew you would see you and tell someone else, who would then feel driven to call you, to see what he had been missing, and the two of you out on a date would be seen by . . .—the result is obvious. I never met people I knew while out on a date, but my mother rejoiced whenever I had one.

In the morning Celeste phoned. "What was wrong with you? You didn't say a word all evening."

"I was nervous."

"You are so inhibited! A congenital ghetto Jew!"

We went again to the little French restaurant, and I was relaxed enough to notice that all that was spoken was French. Esther and I were observers again till Celeste, trying to use a prosaic word, made an outrageous mistake. A burst of laughter, from the boys, rocked our table. A *pompon rouge,* older and strikingly handsome, turned from the table beside us and asked Christophe to tell him the joke. Celeste, pleased, answered for herself, brightly though softly, in French, "Why are they laughing? All I said was . . .," and she repeated it.

The sailor smiled. "Perhaps one day I will explain it, but not now." As he told the joke at his table, laughter erupted not only there, but quickly again at ours.

Neither Esther nor I were sure what Celeste had said, but we surmised enough. I was insulted for Celeste by the excessive laughter, and angry at Christophe, though not at the two for whom I had never had high expectations. Tears filled my eyes, and my tongue was unlocked.

"Christophe, I thought you were a gentleman. Celeste thinks you are, and says you are, so why do you laugh?"

They all fell silent. Then Henri, beside me, said, "But you do speak French."

"Of course I speak French! I just couldn't get it started."
I turned again on Christophe. "What she was trying to tell
you was . . .," and I supplied not only the innocuous word
Celeste had meant, but the whole idea, which I had understood, which I had anticipated, because she was my friend,
and the words emerged from my mouth as for years they
had emerged on paper, in perfect order, with perfect grammar.

Christophe turned to Celeste. "I apologize for my laughter." Then, to me, he said, "Forgive me."

I would have forgiven him anything.

Now that I could speak, Christophe drew me out, and
all the years of conjugating verbs irregular and regular came
to a strange fruition. French was the delicate nose I hadn't
been born with. It was the lindy-hop I hadn't learned. At a
time when a girl had to hide her brain, it was a product of
the brain I could reveal, because it was only a language,
and it was their language—knowing it was normal. We
weren't talking Marx or Veblen, or even Corneille. But
French, my particular French, had worth, and I with it, not
only in the eyes of teachers, but to these boys, who mattered more, and our trivial talk in a restaurant assumed a
supreme importance.

When I arrived at home, I may have seemed subdued, but
I was happier then than I had ever been before.

"You have another date?" my mother asked.

"Yes. Next Saturday."

"All six together again?"

"Celeste and her boy friend, and Henry and I. The other

boy can't make it, so Esther's out."

"Furloughs are short," my father said. "Go to sleep. You have school tomorrow."

How could I sleep?

That week I spent as little time as possible at home. I said I was doing research, and I stayed at school until the library closed for the night. I had only coffee and broth, and the fat fell away from my frame so fast that by Saturday morning my clothes didn't fit. My mother, amazed, said, "All of a sudden you're losing your baby fat. Overnight!" and bought me a dress.

When I met Celeste at the subway, she said, "Christophe phoned with a change of plans. We're going to meet at a bar."

"But I don't drink. I've told you that."

"Neither does he. What you do is order a Coke."

"Then why go there?"

"Henri can't come, so Christophe is bringing someone else, and this new guy wants us to meet at the bar."

"Celeste, I wish you had told me."

"They're not white slavers! What's going to happen?"

What happened was that Christophe was at the bar, not drinking, beside a uniformed man who was, and the man was the sailor who had asked about Celeste's mistake.

"*Enchanté*," he said, but he offered his arm to Celeste. "I won you in a card game," he told her. "That is, I won the right to ask if you would accompany *me* this evening, so that I might have the pleasure of answering your question. You have the right to refuse, naturally, but I hope, chérie, you will not."

Celeste was delighted. She ordered a Scotch, and I mumbled, "A Coke."

When the drinks were ready, Christophe took his and mine to a table, while Celeste and Michel remained at the bar.

"What's wrong?" Christophe asked. "You're disappointed to be with me instead of with Henri?"

"Of course not."

"You're disappointed that it's me and not Michel?"

"It's you who are disappointed. You both wanted Celeste, but for whatever reason—and I don't believe that story about a card game—you got stuck with me. I'm miserable." There was no boy I ever had known to whom I would then have given so honest an answer.

"You haven't understood at all," he said. "Henri could have come, but Celeste would refuse to be paired with Henri. I asked Michel along for her, so that I could be with you. Let Michel explain the word she used. Let them drink their whisky. Tomorrow you and I will go out by ourselves. I want not only to take you to your door, as Henri has done, but to call for you and be introduced to your parents. Do you understand?"

What could I tell my parents? In choosing me above Celeste he had raised me to a status higher than I had ever known. I could not have revealed to anyone what I now felt for Christophe.

"He's taking you out again?" my mother asked.

"Henry didn't show up. I don't think he cared for me."

"So what did you do? Two girls and one fella."

"There were two. Celeste's brought somebody else."

"And this one likes you?"

"I think he does. He's picking me up here tomorrow."

"This one has more character," my father said.

And from my mother, "Pick out a dress. I'll get up early and take it in in the sides, so it doesn't hang like a bag."

I had intended to tell them that he probably wasn't Jewish and argue the whole thing out, but they were making it hard to argue. By morning, I thought I had better postpone the discussion. My mother, squinting, was pinning a seam at my hip when I saw there was something, one thing, she had to be told in advance.

"He doesn't speak English, so I'll have to translate."

"What does he speak?"

"French." My mother stopped pinning and waited. "He's not a sailor, but now, during the war, he works in the merchant marine. They have to be in New York a few weeks, so he's taken a job—he's a baker."

My mother straightened up, appalled. "Frenchmen are mostly Gentiles," she said.

"I haven't asked him. It's premature. It's a silly question for a first date."

"It's not silly at all. How did Celeste's boy friend meet a Frenchman?"

"All the boys are French—it's a complicated story."

"Go call up Celeste and see if she knows."

"I can't call Celeste today. I don't know if she has a date, and if she doesn't and I do, she'll feel terrible."

"Then I want you to ask the boy yourself, today."

Christophe used the elaborate French construction, "It is an honor and a pleasure for me, Madame, Monsieur, to make your acquaintance." I translated freely, "Happy to meet you." I don't know whether my father suspected foul play in this brief translation, or whether it was the name Christophe that disturbed him, but he muttered a strangled "Likewise."

My mother, half-listening, was undone by the mixed bouquet Christophe had brought for her and the one red rose for me. She didn't know the symbolism of the single rose. She looked from the flowers in her hands to the one in mine, shaking her head. "It's not necessary, flowers— tell him. It's not necessary at all."

He understood. "But it is for me a great pleasure," he said at once, and this I translated literally without adding "he says." My mother looked baffled. I think she didn't know whose pleasure I had meant—his or mine.

Christophe—questioning—looked toward the sofa and then at me, but I took his arm, said good-bye to my parents and hurried us out. We were hand in hand as we left the building.

"Christophe, I'm Jewish," I said.

"I'm Catholic. What would you like to do today?"

"Learn to roller skate."

"If that's what would please you, of course."

That day I learned to skate. Christophe's eyes were my mirror, and I knew that if I had ever been clumsy, now I was not.

That night, before he left me, he said there was something of great importance that he and I should discuss. He had a girl in France. He no longer was sure how he felt about her. He had gone with some girls who didn't matter, but now, with me. Danielle expected him to marry her, and maybe he should write and break it off. "Anne, I could not deceive you by telling you nothing about her. I'm too uncertain to break it off, and I can't in a letter, it's cruel, not until I see her at home. So can we still go on together, you and I?"

"I can," I said.

"Did you ask him?" my mother said.

"He's a Catholic. He's engaged to a girl in France, and his ship will be leaving in less than a month. We're only going out together, nothing else."

"Engagements get broken," she said. "He's nice. You'll fall in love. You won't be able to stop yourself, because he's a Frenchman. Flowers! Here who brings flowers? For a prom a boy brings flowers, but otherwise?"

"How will it look?" my father asked. "You'll meet someone we know, and as soon as they hear him talk they'll know what he is. I ask you, how will it look?"

I let even that go by. "Pa, listen. I never went to a prom. There was only one boy in high school that I cared about, but not even one cared about me."

"No!" my mother said. "You have to give him up. The war will be over, and the boys will come home. My butcher has a nephew, a furrier, a good-looking boy, he wants to meet you. You're young. You have plenty of time to look. You don't need to settle for a Gentile boy."

"Settle? Who do you think he is? Some jerk like the ones you keep pushing me to meet? From the Queen of Sheba to Rosa Luxemburg, to have Christophe would not have been to settle! Christophe is *nobody's* compromise."

My mother's rough hands flew to the sides of her head. "God in heaven," she said, "Anne, do you hear yourself talking? Hear how you're *talking* about him."

"I could have lied to you. There are plenty of Jews in France—I could have said Celeste was arranging. . . ."

"Sssssssstop!" she said. "Never say that name to me again. She is my enemy. She is my biggest, my worst enemy."

After those words, my mother stopped talking to me.

The following morning, I saw she wasn't talking to my father either. He was by no means supporting my position, but she had entered upon a mourning of her own devising that barred speech. I said I no longer had to remain at school in the evening. I thought if I'd just come home to dinner, we could work the whole thing out, but during dinner she wouldn't speak. Nor did she eat. She stationed herself at the kitchen sink and skipped her evening meal. Had I been clever enough to do the same, I'd have won.

Instead, I ate again at the college cafeteria—or rather, there I didn't eat, because, while the previous week I hadn't wanted to, now I couldn't.

Celeste understood. Late in the week she said, "Anne, don't lose any more weight. He'll think that you're a consumptive." I smiled. *"Zut alors!"* she said, "she can smile! Look, my clothes will fit you now. I have a new dress Christophe has never seen and I've already worn for Michel. Borrow it."

I shook my head and studied her face. She wasn't even aware of what she already had given to me. She was happy with Michel, and she didn't resent my having Christophe. She had been hinting all that week that there would be a far more intimate relationship between Michel and her than I would have with Christophe, but I refused to acknowledge the hints. I wanted to believe Celeste was perfect, and to me, *that* would have been less than perfect.

On Friday, I left for home immediately after classes. Neighbors of ours were sitting in front of the building.

"Your mother's sick?" I was asked. "She hasn't been out all week."

My mother was sitting alone in the kitchen, where no one could ask her the cause of her grief. I went to the radio, and when I turned it on, she left the room. I phoned Christophe and said he was not to come for me the following evening—that we would meet in the city instead.

We walked to Central Park and sat on a bench, and I told him about my mother. "Christophe, you have Danielle, but I have only you. I've never had anyone but you." I drew away from him to see his eyes. "You asked what you should do about Danielle. Now I'm asking you about my mother."

"I didn't ask if I should hurt Danielle. I said I couldn't do it, yet. I only asked if you'd go on with me. About your mother it's you who must decide, because it's you who are suffering."

"And you apparently are not. If I give you up, it won't matter to you."

"When you got angry at me for laughing at Celeste, it shocked me, but it didn't hurt me, because what you said was fair. This hurts me." I started to apologize, but he knew what I would say, and he covered my lips with his fingers. "Sh . . ., it's not necessary, *mon chou*. Listen. If we do marry, I'll become a Jew. I'm not religious, and whether they call me Jew or Gentile doesn't matter to me if it solves the problem. Tell her that."

"Do you know what that would involve?"

"A bit of skin? It doesn't matter."

In all that time, it hadn't occurred to me that he would agree to this, much less that he would suggest it.

That night, though my parents were waiting up, they were in their room where, presumably, they wouldn't be faced with talking to me, and when I passed their door, the light in their room went out.

In the morning, I told my mother, "I've spoken to Christophe, and if you're right, if we ever decide to marry, he'll become a Jew."

Again, as when I had said he was French, she was appalled.

"Isn't that all right?" I asked.

"No!"

"Why not? You said he was nice."

"He'll be nice till you fight over something. Then he'll know he's a Gentile again, and to him you'll be only a Jew."

I couldn't tell Christophe she would think this way of him, so I decided to tell him only as much as he asked.

"Is it all right?" he said.

"No. She's afraid, and I can't change her mind."

He took my hand. "I understand," he said. "She doesn't know me, so she thinks I'll seduce you and leave you. You can't blame her for that. Let's not talk about it any more. Whatever you decide will be what's right, and I'll accept it. But until you decide, I want to forget. I want to be happy."

I put my mother out of my mind.

Still, when Christophe was not beside me, seeing my mother was hard. Not only was she in mourning—she was aging before my eyes.

On Saturday morning I went with Christophe by bus to a park far from the city. We had a marvelous day, joyous, sensual, but by the standards of the eighties innocent. In the late afternoon, under a tree, I said, "This is our last day."

He winced and drew away from me. I touched his arm.

"Leave me alone," he said.

"You said it was I who had to decide, and you would accept it."

He turned his face even further away. Then he said, "I accept it." He stood up slowly and held out his arms. Solemnly, he said, "I want to remember this day, and I want to remember laughter. Something to make us laugh. Something crazy." He looked around, and soon he pointed. "There. That hill. Let's run down that hill."

Alarmed, I said, "That's not a hill. That's more like a precipice. We'll get killed."

He appraised the hill again. "You're too timid. It will be fun. *Le bon Dieu* in whom I don't believe, He watches over the young, *n'est-ce pas?*"

Suddenly I was being pulled along the road against my will. "Christophe, no, I don't want to. I'm afraid. There's nothing funny about it—it's dangerous."

"It isn't. I'll protect you, I'll hold you. I'm strong, and I'm not afraid," and we were running down the hill, unable to control our speed, my hand in his, though he was a little in front of me. The ground was rutted and strewn with rocks, and there was nothing to grab to slow us down. A shrub—jagged and sharp—reared up before us, but instead of stopping us it separated us and passed us. Alone now, I felt my knees begin to crumble, and all I knew was me, my safety, my life. Christophe was gone from my mind for longer, it seemed, than we had lived, till all at once he reappeared, and we had reached the sudden, slamming bottom of the hill and found our pace was slowing, slowing, and that we were finally alive and upright on the flat miraculous ground.

He threw his arms around me, and he shouted above my head to some vengeful god, "You see? You could not kill us! We are young! We are happy! *Nous sommes immortels!*"

That word is fixed for me forever in his voice and accent. Whenever I have to say "immortal," I have to stop and think and translate.

I tore myself away to catch my breath and kiss him. Tears were trickling out of his eyes, and his mouth was stretched in a failed smile. "I'm not crying," he said. "I'm laughing, you see? *Je ris.*"

Savagely he dried his tears, and moments later we sat on the grass. He took a package out of his coat and gave it to me. "A present," he said.

It was a silver compact, elegant, finer than any I had ever held, a field of flowers etched on the lid. Inscribed on the back were our names, and inside it was a slip of paper with Christophe's Bordeaux address.

"I planned to hold it for you," he said, "till just before I was going to sail. If you have something new to tell me, write. And I, when I have seen Danielle, will know what I must write to you."

That night I told my mother I had said good-bye to Christophe. She slowly sat down on a kitchen chair and, covering her face with her hands, sobbed.

Celeste continued to see Michel, so I knew when the Riche- lieu left port, but I didn't find out about the ship Chris- tophe was on. I never heard from Christophe, and I didn't write to him because there was nothing new to say.

Celeste and I were friends till graduation. Then, in a quarrel over a boy she took away from me before we could see he wasn't worth taking, our friendship ended.

About two years later, on the subway platform, I met Leon. He was still living with Celeste's mother, and we talked about Celeste, who was away at graduate school, about me, and then he said, suddenly, "'Anne, I'm sorry about Christophe."

I wasn't going to sound regretful to Leon and let him report it to Celeste, so I said, *"Don't* be. There were too many cultural differences between Christophe and me, so it didn't matter."

"But Christ!" he said. "You didn't want him dead!"

Celeste, in a final act of friendship, had spared me the news.

It wasn't only Christophe. It was Henri as well, and oth- ers. Michel, who like Christophe was from Bordeaux, had written to Celeste, long afterward. Henri was sixteen.

I didn't ask Leon how. In that minute on the subway platform, it didn't occur to me. Later, when it did, what was the use?

A train came. "Go, Leon, go," I said. "I'll take the next one." He was reluctant to leave me standing alone. "Go! I want to be by myself."

Even on that day, as on the day I had said good-bye to Christophe, I wasn't angry at my mother. Except for the time she had belittled Christophe with the word "settle," I was never angry.

It wasn't until we learned about the camps that I fully understood my parents' fear of Gentiles. I was twenty then, but another twenty years were to pass before I began to question my parents' demands and my own compliance. It was then I was angry at them, but the greater anger, by far, was against myself.

Giant Sequoia

I jog this route every day, and several times a week—somewhere—I find a penny. Sometimes two. I stash them away, and when Robert and I decide The Time to Try has finally come, I'll have gathered enough for a package of Pampers. Robert, however, believes that when I stoop for pennies, cerebral cells escape through my ears.

Today I found a dime. Some evil benefactor is at large, stalking this dim-witted Gretel. Tomorrow I must bring along the chicken bone.

Over a nightcap, I show my parents my cache—an hour ago they arrived from New York. They've entrusted their plants to their friends but brought their neuroses, which they think they hide from us in innocent questions.

My mother: "You jog by yourself? Robert doesn't go along?"

Robert, tenderly, as if he's discovered she's senile: "Remember, Mom? Bonnie jogs? Robert swims?"

My father: "Don't talk to her like that. From Howie we *never* hear such disrespect."

Robert's glance is resentful, but his voice respectful. "Because nothing that doesn't affect him offends him."

My dad resists any further talk of my sister's husband. "So. So Rob, tell me, just how integrated *is* this town?"

"Very, Archie."

My father, who was accustomed as a child to putdowns from his parents, now accepts the putdowns from his kids. He sips his kir, and Rob, with a quick shake of his head, shifts mental gears and is back in Normal, where he can remember that generally he and they are on the same side.

"Tomorrow, Bonnie," my mother says, "before we leave for Sequoia, instead of jogging, take me out to that Foothills Park." But then in the morning she says, "As long as we're driving, why don't you show me the streets where you jog."

"Why?" I ask, hopping onto Robert's bandwagon. "It's too early for blacks to be up and about." My mother clams up. "I was kidding," I say. "These are the streets where I jog." She's still silent, so I—guilty but with an explanation—add, "I was imitating Rob."

"For ten years! Why don't you imitate Leontyne Price? Who has some *respect* for her mother."

I refuse to get into Comparative Racial Parental Respect. "This is the street where I've found most of the pennies," I tell her, as if she has reason to care, "and at the next intersection I found the dime."

But at the next intersection, at a corner house, is a man who is wearing a purple sweatshirt and Abraham Lincoln's father's jeans. His hands are on his hips, he's surveying the street, and he's big and young and very black.

My mother says, "Oh, God."

"That's Martin Luther Freeman," I say. "He's an M.D./ Ph.D. at Lockheed." My mother searches my face. "Didn't Robert tell you?" I ask. "They have a Space Medicine group. I wish *Rob* could work there, instead of in a junior high."

"Oh," she says, "well,'" and shrugs in sympathy, but then at breakfast she says, "Rob? We saw Martin Luther Freeman."

"Who? Oh oh oh oh, for God's sake," he says. "When did we see him last, Bonnie—at the Poppovitches' party?"

"Poppovitch," my father repeats, chuckling.

Robert places a bulky block on top of the stack: "Helmut Poppovitch from eastern East Germany. Escaped to the West. What did you think of Martin, Mom? Did you stop and talk?"

My father's chuckling stopped a dozen syllables back.

"Robert," my mother says, "I know my daughter's smart. Smart she got from her genes. Smart-alecky she got from you."

"Okay, Mom," he says, "we're sorry. No more." Then he asks, "Bonnie, who *did* you see?"

"I don't know. Someone probably weeding his lawn."

My mother: "Who would be weeding his lawn seven o'clock Sunday morning you hardly can see in the fog?"

Rob: "Someone trying to sell his house."

"Someone trying to see your wife! Someone who knows she goes jogging alone!"

Robert snaps his fingers. "The dimedropper! He likes to see my Bonnie bent over."

My father erupts. "Robert!"

"Oh, come on, Dad," I say. "And since we're on the subject of being bent over, did you notice that although he does, I admit, say 'ass,' he never uses those associated other words that so offend you, so why don't you ever appreciate *that?*"

My mother says, "I don't know why we came."

My father says, "I'm glad no one else is hearing my children's stupid remarks."

His summary's right, but Robert's insulted. As I walk to the sink, he tells me, "Leave them! I'll do them myself."

"Why?" I ask. "You cooked, I wash.'"

"I'll let you make it up," he says. "'When *my* parents come, I'll let you wash the floors."

By the time my father has turned from Rob to my mother, her eyes are back from on high, and she says, "Bonnie, how can you live with this man?"

"Mom," says Robert softly, "You really like me a lot. So does Dad." No one laughs or Oh-sures. Or even looks incredulous. What he's said hangs in the silence, an invisible and yet a visible truth. "You may not think me as big a success," he says, "but you like me better anyway. You know?"

They know. They understand his use of the comparative and know to whom he refers. Their other son-in-law, whose Sunday brunches could feed Ethiopia, who once knew all about children of war and now knows only the noses of wine, is the one they'd rather talk about than to—though they don't admit it to Rob.

I wish I could break the silence with something outrageous but equally true, and thereby elicit a laugh.

My father is sitting up front with Rob. This, he believes, is his due for having to watch the road on vacations when I was a child while the "women" were seeing the sights. I'm careful not to remind him that I, in fact, never saw anything either. While *he* was doing the driving, *I* was throwing up.

We approach the important corner, and there, still—or again—is my Martin Luther Freeman. My mother: "Rob! There!"

We've passed him, so Robert slows, looks in the rearview mirror, stops, and puts the car in reverse.

My mother, whose jaws are securely locked, says, "Rahahb, what *are* you *doing?*"

He drives backward in a clean straight line. "Pardon me," he calls out, "is Loma Verde anywhere near here?"

The man sets his loppers on the ground, comes to the curb and says, "It's parallel to here a quarter mile away, but—because of all these semicircles—drive a little further, and follow the curve of the street. It intersects with Ross. Turn left, go two blocks and you're there. The freeway's east to your right, El Camino's west to your left."

"Thanks," says Rob.

"Thanks," echoes my father.

My mother nods and smiles, as grateful as if he had given us lunch.

"A very articulate man," says my father.

Rob: "You thought he would answer in grunts?"

"Listen," says my mom, "stop acting as if we were bigots."

"Me?" says Robert the innocent. "I just wanted you to meet him and be reassured. Why do you always misread me?"

My mother, now uncertain, tells him she's sorry.

"Now that you've seen he's handsome and articulate," he adds, "you won't feel bad if she does get raped."

My mother opens her handbag and snatches a comb. She runs it through her hair a single time on each side of an imaginary part. This response is a benign condition called Bonnie's Tic, named for the then ten-year-old neurologist, who discovered it in Gloria, her mother, whenever Gloria undergoes stress.

My mother has not considered this last remark funny at all. I can see, though I should have seen it earlier, that Robert has gone entirely too far. I touch my mother's hand, but she doesn't respond. Her head is directed forward and fixed in place, as if an artist with little scissors were cutting her profile from golden foil.

Rob stops for gas, and as he walks to the pump my mother says, "Leonard, I want to go home."

"Home?"

"New York.'

"Oh, Gloria," he says, kindly, in a way that makes her name an endearment. "But you *know* that boy by now."

"I don't. Neither one of them—or the whole generation of them. They're still inventing justice and love."

"We didn't mean to be disparaging," I say. "We meant you shouldn't be so afraid of *people*."

"Why not? Who causes trouble? Chipmunks?"

"The man was standing in front of his house, and you were ready to think the worst."

"I can't talk to you, Bonnie. I'd like to go home."

"Not like this—I can't let you, and you know it. It won't happen again."

"Can you speak for your husband too?" my father asks.

"He won't say another word."

"You'll tell him not to?" my mother asks. "Thanks! You'll make him resentful, you'll ruin your marriage, and who'll get the blame?—*me*."

"Stop playing those tapes! And don't tell me how to deal with my husband."

Robert looks in at the window, anxious, and my parents shut up: he's not a son, only a son-in-law, so he isn't supposed to know that we fight.

Robert goes off to pay for the gas, and when he gets back my parents and I are dormant, each encased in an angry cocoon. He lets himself back in the car, looks in the rearview mirror and says, "Mom, I'm sorry."

My mother shakes her head awhile and answers at last, "You know who *I'm* sorry for, Robert? Your parents."

Neither Rob nor I will reveal that *his* parents are sorry for mine.

Fully reconciled, we are now in Sequoia National Park. My mother had not yet seen a full-blooded coastal redwood, much less a giant sequoia, and she is hanging half way out the window, her head turned up and her cultured pearls slapping the side of our yellow Corolla.

"Stop! Pull off! Let me out! I can't see up to the top!"

"Wait," I say, "this is nothing. Wait till we get to the Giant Forest."

But Robert gives in. He parks on the gravel with only a simple "A minute, Mom, hear?"

My father stays in the car with Rob. My mother, her purse dangling from her shoulder, picks her way on two-and-a-half inch heels through the forest debris. She stops and arches backward, trying to see to the tops of the trees. She crosses her wrists on her chest and grasps her upper arms.

"Oooh, oooh," she murmurs. "Never—never in all my life."

Here, under this venerable tree, whose distinctions are that it is huge and ancient and alive and beautiful, she is as overcome as I—only weeks before—under the dome of Saint Peter's in Rome. I wish my father and Robert were seeing her too.

When we came to this park by ourselves, Robert and I rented a primitive cabin. It had the world's most terrible beds, a porch with a wood-burning stove, and—one early morning—a little yellow bird asleep, its head under its wing. But the beds in the cabins are not for the backs of sixtyish parents, so now we have chosen the lodge.

As we leave our room, I reinstruct my husband: "Not one derisive word, you hear?"

He bows his head submissively and says, "Mein Führer."

My mother has changed into sneakers, a wraparound skirt and a shirt with a pocket containing her change-purse— which is really a kind of emergency kit. It has an I.D. with numbers of next-of-kin, a handkerchief (tissues don't convert to tourniquets), an inch of comb, a twenty dollar bill (so that a mugger won't kill her out of sheer rage), several dimes for the use of a phone, and assorted other change.

Some wonderful hours go by. My mother has gazed at the General Sherman, wished that a tree so great had never been given that dreadful name, climbed to the top of Moro Rock, admired the clever abode Mr. Tharp built in a log, mourned the fallen sequoias, craned her neck at hundreds of branches, and she is now so much at home among the trees that she can take her eyes from them when one of us talks. She visits the giant sequoias now as she visits her aged aunts—proud of how well they're doing but very protective—and as she stands again near the General Sherman, a little black girl appears, climbs over the rail and runs to the base of the tree.

Returning, the child approaches us, and my mother asks her, "Darling? Come back over the fence—please? Don't run over the roots any more—it's bad for the tree—okay?"

The little girl remains on the other side of the railing and soon, her eyes revealing her suspicion of my mother, scampers toward her family, some twenty feet away.

My father says to my mother, "Who asked you to save the trees? James Watt?"

"Who taught you to be such a comic? Rob?"

The child is happily running from railing to tree and back, and my mother's becoming upset. The black family is clearly not—and has decided, in fact, that there is some pressing business awaiting them closer to us. The couple I think are the parents are thirty or less—a little bit younger than Robert and I—and they're part of a group of eight.

As the child comes near again, the woman says, "That's right, Royanne. You don't have to do what she says."

My mother becomes as still as she was when the scorn she heard was from Robert and me. Seconds go by, and then she looks, as do we all, at the woman—at her fine brown face and cornrowed hair with its intricate pattern of woven-in beads.

"Why not?" my mother says. "I didn't ask for something for myself. They put in a fence. The signs are asking us nicely. I think she should learn some respect for the tree."

Languidly a slender teenage girl comes forward, saunters over to my mother and laughs. "Had a good look?" she asks.

"Yes."

"Got any more to say?"

"Yes. You're trying to say you're as good as me? *That* I found out long ago, when I knew you as negroes, before you were born and were told you're black. Just remember you're also as bad."

The girl reflects for a second, tosses back her head and laughs. Hoots! My mother never had an audience this good, and now the others in the group are laughing at her too.

Half the United States' caucasians happen to be here, but no one is venturing close. The laughers turn their backs at last, but my mother doesn't budge until the last of them has gone. An older woman, pink and blond, hurries forward now, and in an intimate tone that implies she would like to hear from one of genuine us some tidbit proving that *we* have always been right about *them*, asks, "What did they do?"

"Nothing," my mother says. "What business is it of yours?"

The woman retreats, her perfect nose, however, at an angle that shows she's sure whatever my mother got she deserved.

Robert turns and walks away. I see my mother open her change-purse and know she will reach for her fragment of comb. I want to say something kind, but before I can, she says, "Go, Bonnie, go with Rob. We'll catch up."

I do as she asks, but when I get to Rob he says, "I feel rotten." He stops, and we wait for my parents to reach us. "Say it, Mom," he says.

My mother looks puzzled. "What should I say?"

"You've had a bad day, so say whatever you like."

"But about what?"

"You know?" he says. "If I hadn't met Bonnie first, I'd have tried to get married to *you*."

She only half-smiles, as if she's expecting a wise-crack to follow and, when it doesn't, she says, "Oh-sure. Harold and Maude, Robert and me. You were *meant* to be my son-in-law."

He considers her answer, and then, softly, he says, "Your *better* son-in-law."

For a moment she's taken aback. Then, "So what should I do for you?" she asks. "Make you some blintzes?"

Coaxing, as if he's been giving her clues and she hasn't caught on, "But *why* am I better?" he asks.

"Because when *he* argues, *when* he argues, it's not over something important."

Robert is so absurdly relieved I'm shocked—he seems to have needed to hear this. Adored by his mother, why does he need to be loved by mine? And why have I never seen this before, where have I been?

"Is that really why?" he asks. "Or is it because when you're with *me* you don't have to feel you're outclassed?"

Now it's my mother who's shocked. She looks as she did when my hippie kid-sister came home with the Klopman diamond. "You think I feel inferior to *his* kind of class?"

"You don't?" he asks. "Even when you're *surrounded* by people like that you don't . . . ." He doesn't seem able to finish without betraying himself even more.

"Robert, you know?" she says. "You ought to get a medal for craziness. Here." She pulls her change-purse out of her pocket and offers a penny. "Here is the medal for craziness. This is the Lincoln medal. Lincoln himself never was crazy, but dimes I need for telephone calls."

Robert, without so much as a pause, holds out his hand, and the penny is his.

Children,
Dogs and
Dying Men

All I wanted with Frank, at first, was that he sell me one of his dogs. I had asked a veterinarian to suggest a Boxer breeder, and he, taking a card from his wallet, said, "A girl alone, too new in town to know what's what—you need a dog that can guard. Frank here, he has Dobermans."

I didn't want a Doberman, but I wasn't accustomed then to insisting on what I wanted. I took the card, fully intending to throw it away, but soon I decided that what he had said made sense.

"One month old?" Frank asked. "You don't take a puppy from its mother till at least six weeks, but come on down, and we can talk about it."

So we talked, or rather Frank did, because I knew nothing, while he knew everything and knew that besides. He put a small black puppy in my hands, gently, and told me a series of stories from over sixty years of breeding and training dogs.

Once, he said, he had called the Pentagon, collect, and ordered General Bradley to return a dog the army no longer needed and would kill—and had gotten it back. A pistol in his hand, he had retrained the dog, and when the animal was "safe," he took it to visit a woman confined to an iron lung.

"The dog fell in love with her," he said, "and when it was time to leave, he wouldn't budge, so I let her have him as a gift. She lived for twelve more years, and you'd think the dog would have died by then, but he didn't. But once that woman was dead, he refused to eat, and all I could do for him then was put him to sleep."

He went on and on. He seemed an epic figure, old, but strong nevertheless, and proud of his audacity. I, who had been shielded—adored by a peaceable father, directed by a powerful mother, enslaved by a grand piano—had hardly had time for girl friends, much less for men, and I surely had never met men who had nerve like Frank's. Sooner than I would have liked, we heard a car in the driveway.

Frank introduced me to Paula, his partner, and Eddie, her husband. Eddie was thirty perhaps, tall and lean, but I couldn't guess Paula's age at all. Her face as that of the grossly obese, pretty in a way, with all its distinguishing angles concealed under plump little cushions. Her body was almost cylindrical—a column to support an overpass.

They had three litters, but no "baby," she said, would be ready to go before two weeks. Soon there'd be another litter from a bitch she had sent back east, where they were having her mated with Caesar.

"Caesar," Frank explained, "belongs to Ilse Koestler. . . ."

Paula stopped him. "She isn't interested in Ilse."

Frank continued, louder, "Once, German-American Bundists wanted dogs, and Ilse told them, 'Show up here, you Nazis, and I'll turn my dogs on you, I. . . .'"

"Diane?" Paula asked. "Do you want a dog or a bitch?"

To my regret, Frank yielded, and I, though annoyed at Paula, thought I shouldn't intrude. "A female," I said.

She handed me a magazine on Dobermans and went for some other puppies, and Eddie followed her out.

"Frank?" I asked. "Are you and Paula related?"

"No. She knew me because of my dogs. Last year, when my wife died, she asked me to live here and make her my partner. It's a nice house. It ought to have kids."

Paula returned, and three black puppies were soon on the floor. I knelt beside them to look at them closely.

"Can you tell them apart?" Frank asked. "In a couple of weeks you will, so wait, and if you can't by then, leave it to me. I mean it, Diane, I'll give you the best." I looked up, surprised, pleased. "You have class," he said. Later, when I rose to leave, he asked me to come there to see him again.

"Meanwhile," Paula said, "this is the T-litter, so come up with a name that starts with a T."

Frank touched my arm. "A *noble* name," he said, "I hate it when a dog of mine is given a foolish name." As I turned to go, he asked, "What do you do for a living, Diane?"

"I teach." He smiled. "Kindergarten," I said.

"I knew you're a teacher. You're what? Twenty-one?"

"Twenty-three."

"I'd have had a granddaughter older than you."

A few days later, encouraged by Frank's invitation, I went there again. Paula greeted me warmly and talked about raising winners. Frank, however, was thinking of something else.

"I was the fourteenth of sixteen kids," he said. "My parents used to have sex, and then kids, and when they had more kids than they could feed, they'd give some away. My little sister and I went to an uncle." He said it without any bitterness and, in fact, with apparent amusement.

The next time, Eddie was again at home. Paula and he appeared to have quarreled, and, trying to be discreet, I turned my attention entirely to Frank.

"Once when I was ten," he said, "I was on the lam from my uncle—I'd missed church, so I knew I'd really catch it at home. I had a friend with me, it was night, on the Bowery, when a drunk came along. A cop came out of a doorway, and in an Irish brogue as good as my father's, he spits out a string of four-letter words." Frank's eyes became distant, and his speech was broken by pauses. "He lifts up his club, and he slams it so hard on the drunk that the skull goes crackkk! . . . Even when the man is falling, again, crackkk! . . . The cop bends down to look, and my friend vomits, and a mutt comes up out of nowhere and sniffs the bloody head, the vomit, the cop's behind. . . . I bet on Sundays the cop went to church."

Paula rose, bringing him back to the present, and as she stalked from the room, he said, "She's offended. I'm sorry."

"For what?" I asked.

Surprised, he started to answer but stopped, and soon he said, "Did I tell you I was excommunicated?"

Eddie answered, "Lots of times."

"I meant Diane," he countered coldly. "A priest talked

my sister into being a nun, and when I got my hands on him, I put him in the hospital." He said it defiantly, and I, hearing him, saw nothing wrong in what he had done.

A few days later, I phoned. "I'd like to see you again," I said. "Am I taking too much of your time?"

"Oh, child," he said, "'what could I do with my time that you think would be better?"

"I can come in the afternoon, tomorrow or the day after."

"Tomorrow. Paula will be at the vet's watching him crop some ears."

The following day he said, "You like to hear about the dogs, don't you?"

"I like to hear about you too."

"Talk is all I'm good for now."

"Talk is fine."

"Then how come you don't talk?"

"I have nothing special to tell. I was never afraid to go home. Nobody cracked a skull in front of my eyes, or cut up my face, as someone apparently did to yours."

He raised a hand and rubbed a scar on his temple close to his eye. "I gave worse than I got. I should have been culled from the litter right from the start."

"Culled?" I asked. "Put to sleep?"

"I killed a man. I was a union organizer, and he was a scab. I heaved him over a balcony, and I never got caught."

It took me a while to speak. "I thought the only work you did was work with dogs."

He studied my face. "Dogs were a sideline. You know what a wainwright is? When I was fourteen I got a job on a ship. Went to Ireland to learn the wainwright's trade. I did a lot of things—construction, ship's carpenter, the union, the war. What about you? There has to be *some*thing."

"Safety, 'culture,' college close to home—my mother owned me as you'd own an expensive pet. She was very good to me but kept me on a short leash. I decided to be a human adult, so I left and came here."

"You're becoming an adult in a kindergarten?"

"Any act of escape—even that—can be intimidating."

"Maybe I didn't have brains enough to be intimidated. I got married at fifteen to a little Irish girl, got her pregnant, put her on a ship to bring her here, but didn't even worry what could happen giving birth on a ship. And they died." With hardly a pause, he added, "You're a pretty girl, and good-natured, nice. Do you have a special boy friend?"

"Not a special one, no."

"Diane, don't let a man push you into something you don't want to do. And don't be angry that I give you advice."

"I'm not angry."

"Diane, do you want to know if I ever got married again?"

"You've said you did and that she died last year."

"I had two others in between."

"Do you want to tell me?"

"I talk a lot, but there are things I've kept inside. I'm over eighty, and yes, I want to tell you."

I didn't know why Frank had chosen me, but I had sought him out, had wanted to hear whatever he'd say, and his simple request made it seem utterly right that I should.

"My second wife had money, and she liked fast cars. One day she took our kids for a drive, and the car hit a tree. She and three of the kids got killed. I took the one that was left and kept him with me wherever I went. The day I killed the scab, my son was asleep in the back of the car, a few feet away. Then I met this girl. She was seven-

teen. I never met anyone smarter. She wanted to be a doctor, and for wanting that, her parents beat her. She was
running away to at least be a nurse. I was making very
good money, and a girl like that, how could I let her clean
bed-pans? She married me. She did her studying, like we
agreed she would, but she also took care of my boy as if
he was a prince." He lifted his eyes to mine. "And when
she became a doctor, I left her, because I couldn't fit in
with her friends." He took a deep breath. "My son was
sixteen. He got angry at me for leaving her, and the minute
he saw me ship out, he signed up. It was World War II,
and the kid lied—said he was older—so the army would
take him. That's the story. That's all."

It was almost too much for me to absorb. "That's all?"
I said at last. "My God, was he killed?"

"It should have been me."

"What are you saying, Frank? Are you blaming yourself?"

"Who else would I blame?"

"But by enlisting, he was hurting not only you, he was
hurting her as well. Wasn't he?"

"Of course. But if *I* was over forty and stupid, you want
my kid sixteen to be smart?"

I tried, but I could find nothing to say to comfort him,
and after a while he said, "It's done. I've told you, and now
we won't discuss it again."

When I went to see him next, he didn't come out of his
room. Paula showed me the dogs, and told me Frank would
be grading the litter soon, but when I went for the puppy
he'd chosen for me, though Eddie was there, Frank was
not.

Filling out forms, Paula asked me the name. I wondered

if I should explain it to her—I had meant to explain it only to Frank. At last I said, "Torr."

"You mean Thor."

"I mean Torr. It means a mountain peak—a summit. I spell it the Irish way with a double 'r'. Please tell Frank."

I thought of Frank repeatedly. I wondered what kind of man he'd have been if he'd had a childhood like mine, and why he had chosen me to be his confessor. I wanted to see him, console him, talk about strength—Frank, is it inborn? chosen? snatched?—but I was convinced that what he had wanted of me was just that I listen, leave and remember. And yet, when six months had passed, I decided to phone.

Paula answered, and after some talk I asked for Frank.

"It's bad when they get dependent," she said, "so now he's living alone."

I asked her for his number, but she said she didn't have it, nor in fact, she said, did she have his address.

There was a listing in the phone book, and I called, but there wasn't any answer. Nor was there any the following day, a Saturday, so with Torr in the car I went looking for him.

It was an area often reported about, where teen-agers, and even pre-teens, were routinely harrassing the aged. The house where Frank was living was dismal, and seven or eight young men were out, lounging against an adjacent fence. They turned to stare, and I stayed in the car for a minute, trying to guess what they meant to do.

I took some paper out of the glove box and scribbled a

note. With Torr at my side, I walked to the house, knocked, and after a while, shoved the paper under the door.

The following morning, Frank phoned. He had been in Sacramento, judging a show, and when I asked if I might visit, he suggested we meet somewhere else, for coffee, instead.

"The money," he said, as the waitress seated us, "the reputation, the bitches on breeders' contracts, everything was mine, but when she sold the puppies she and Eddie kept the money. Worse, they kept the pedigrees, and when I said I need the pedigrees or I can't make a living, Eddie told me, 'Go on welfare.' " He paused for a moment. "When I was young, Diane—you should have seen me—I'd have bent him in half with my hands. But now, when you came to the house, he could lock me up in my room."

"Frank, I'm sorry," I said. "I didn't know."

"They say I'm senile, I embarrass them. If I were senile, would I remember you told them a torr is a peak? A summit. Noble. You spell it the Irish way, with a double 'r'."

"Frank, you can fight them—I'll go with you. We'll get a lawyer and go to court."

"Fight? At my age? I'm not at home in courts. And I'm not on welfare either. I'll start all over."

"How? You need the pedigrees."

"I'll go to people who bought my dogs and copy from theirs. If you make mistakes, you have to pay."

"But for me it would be easy to go to court. I want to. I've never had to fight in all my life, against anyone."

"You never had to fight?" He laughed softly, briefly. "I know you're young, Diane, but never?"

"There wasn't any need. Or what little need there was, somebody else did it for me."

"That must be nice," he said. He became thoughtful awhile. "But you see?" he said, "the ones who did your fighting for you, it's them you should have fought."

He meant it as food for thought, of course, but coming as it did, so unexpectedly, I couldn't ingest it, or touch it, or even look at it. A fork-lift truck could not have lifted the weight of it. But I could handle the morsel about mistakes and payment, and I did as soon as I left him.

It was like Torr with raisins. She could eat a quart of food a minute, but a raisin required forever. I would drop one for her on the kitchen floor and, hearing it fall, she'd leap out of bed and race for it, as if expecting that I would compete. The raisin captured, she would mouth it, chew it, get it stuck on a tooth, laboriously work it free, transfer it, chew again, lose, search, find, savor, swallow, chew again in recollection, lick her lips in retrospect—a banquet.

That was how I masticated the cliché about mistakes. I wondered why, when I heard Frank tell about the priest he had battered, I hadn't cared about the priest. I had cared about the man he had killed, but not enough to damage my esteem for Frank. It was a matter of debts. The rich pay debts when they find it convenient, but Frank had had to pay in advance, at usurious rates, and I didn't want him to pay any more. But he had refused to let me fight, and as I moved the morsel around in my mind, I found I was feeling relieved, because he had freed me of all obligation.

For a week. It was Saturday morning again, and I was getting ready for a day of hiking in the foothills, when I recalled, ". . . the ones who did your fighting for you, it's them. . . ." In the time that Torr would need to bolt her dinner, I perceived that there were no excuses now. Without phoning Frank, I went directly to his house.

"Diane!" he said. "I forgot you were coming."

"You didn't forget. I didn't tell you. The fault's mine."

He moved aside and let me in. The room was large, but overwhelmingly dingy. Only one of its walls was newly painted, and on that one were plaques, framed portraits of dogs, and shelves with dozens of trophies.

"Frank, we didn't talk about the Kennel Club. If you told the club what happened, wouldn't they intervene?"

"Maybe."

"Then let's come up with a letter and send it today."

"No. Never. Making a scandal would hurt the breed."

"After all you've been through you'll live like this? At least bluff! Make Paula *believe* that you'll write it."

"You're a good girl, Diane, but about dogs, Paula knows me better than you do."

Before I left, I gave him a card with my name and number to keep in his wallet. I went to the vet who had sent me to him, and without explaining I asked for—and he gave me—a list of Doberman breeders and vets. Then at home, I typed a letter to the Kennel Club, reporting what Paula and Eddie had done to Frank.

I took the letter and lists, drove to Paula's and parked at the curb, and even before the ignition was off, barking began in the closed garage. A car was in the driveway, and as I passed it, I detected heat from under the hood, and knew that Eddie or Paula, or both, had only just arrived. Through the noise from the dogs I could hear them inside—quarreling. Trained in politeness, I turned to leave. Then I reconsidered and approached the door. The voices were loud and the subject unmistakable.

"Don't *call* me that," Paula shouted. "I'm trying!"

"You're eating! The minute no one's watching you, you're

eating. You *are* a pig. You need a trough and slops!"

There was a sudden burst of objects breaking, shattering, and Paula pleaded, "Eddie, please, no more. I do whatever else you want. Don't I *always* do whatever you want?"

I couldn't hear Eddie's response. I heard him move to the door, and I backed away as he flung it wide. I glimpsed Paula, half-way across the kitchen, distraught.

Eddie, seeing me, showed no discomfort or even surprise, but closed the door and approached me. "How *about* that?" he asked.

"I've come to talk about Frank," I said.

"What about him?"

"You owe him money, and you have his pedigrees."

"He slept and ate here, so I don't owe him. And I don't have his pedigrees, but if I did, he couldn't use them anyway, he's senile." He passed me, climbed into his car and drove away.

I wondered if Paula had come to the door to listen. Had it been I, humiliated, I would have fled, and I decided to go on as if she had done precisely that. I rang the bell. The dogs, though I hadn't noticed, had stopped their barking, and now they started again. Mildly interested, I counted the voices. Four. Suddenly, I thought of Ilse Koestler's warning, "I'll turn the dogs on you." Now I was afraid.

Torr was mine, and I loved her, but I would never trust her alone with a mischievous child. I had seen a readiness to strike, to retaliate, just below the surface of her charm. And she was so aware of me and of my moods that when I once had shed some tears while reading, she had climbed all over me, nuzzling my cheeks, peering into my eyes, imploring me not to be sad. I was convinced she'd kill if anyone caused me real distress, and the Dobermans here were Paula's.

I didn't know whether the dogs were enclosed in pens or roaming about. I could picture Paula, opening the garage, setting them free. I could hardly breathe. Nor could I let myself leave. Though I was vulnerable, so was Paula, wounded by Eddie's insults and by her own suspicion that I had heard them, and only when she was vulnerable could I hope to win for Frank. I rang again. The dogs were raging, and from the brushing sounds of their pads, I knew they were loose.

Paula was with them. "Nestor, Pandora, come! Orestes, sit! Stay!" The barking subsided. The garage door opened upward, and Paula emerged.

"I'd like to come in," I said. "I'd like to talk."

"Today is not convenient for me."

"I know. I've been at the door since Eddie got home, and I heard. But it has to be now."

"What do you want to talk about?"

"Eddie."

She turned to the open garage as if looking for safety, but stopped. She looked about inside, as if decisions were physical things and could therefore be found. At last she lifted her hand and slowly pulled the garage door down.

She approached me cautiously and led me into the house. From the entry hall I saw, on the kitchen floor, pink ice cream, chocolate syrup like an oil slick above it, and pools of a carbonated beverage, the few remaining bubbles reflecting fragments of light.

"What *about* Eddie?" she asked.

"Eddie doesn't know what I would do. I asked him for what you owe Frank, and. . . ."

"Frank? You said about Eddie."

"I'm telling you. Eddie doesn't know me. You'd never show another dog. I'll send this letter to the Kennel Club— read it. This list of breeders, this list of vets—they'll all get copies. I'll compromise about the money, but you're giving back the pedigrees."

She walked to a living-room chair and let herself drop down in it. Soon she was making ambiguous sounds, sounds of crying that had overtones of laughter. Tears rolled down. I thought she was crying, and that my threat had caused it. Then I thought she might be laughing, because—expecting some grave revelation about Eddie—all she had heard was "pedigrees." She went on, and at last I knew she was crying. With an effort, she stopped. She didn't dry her tears or the film that had run from her nose. Sniffling and shuddering were the only sound and motion. Then these too stopped, and she sat utterly still. Slowly she rose. She made her way around the puddles and broken glass to the door between the kitchen and garage. She released the dogs from the stay command, and when she returned a minute later she was carrying a folder.

"Here," she said, "and don't forget, old maid, *I,* at least, am married."

My knees were trembling hard when I reached my car. I drove away, and minutes later I stopped at the side of the road until I was calm. Then I went to Frank's and handed the folder to him.

"I broke her in half," I said, "as you'd have done to Eddie once."

"You what?"

"I wasn't strong, but *she* was even weaker. I told her a lie, but not about you. About me. I said I'd tell the club."

His shoulders sagged with relief. "You can't get in trouble for *that,*" he said.

"Were you afraid I'd get in trouble?"

"For a minute there, yes."

"But now you're glad I did it?"

"You don't know I'm glad?" he asked. "And why aren't *you?*"

"I am! Oh God, how glad I am."

"But you don't look it. I don't understand you, Diane. *I* want to celebrate. Don't *you?*"

"Frank, I'm glad, but I don't want to celebrate. There was something terribly wrong about this."

"But there always is," he said.

"All right. Celebrate without me tonight. I'll call you tomorrow, and we'll have another party together."

Sunday the phone awoke me. Frank was in the hospital, his wallet had a card, was I a relative? the woman asked.

No, a friend, but what had happened?

An old man, you realize, too heavy a meal at a restaurant. Too much celebration, he'd said—she didn't know why—he had been there alone, there was no one to ask. He was in Coronary Care, and soon, in a couple of hours, I could visit.

I groomed the dog. I brushed and sponged her coat and began on her toenails. She had never liked my cutting her nails, and she started to whine, a continuous whine that was broken only by pauses for breath. When I finished up front and took hold of her left hind leg, she suddenly growled and retracted her lips. I was shocked. "Torr!" I shouted. "Bad dog! Put those lips down!" I pressed my nose to the tip of hers and said, "Put those teeth away, do you hear me?" Her nose, still against mine, her teeth still thoroughly bared, she extended her long wet tongue and licked my lips. Then she brought her own lips forward and resumed her high-pitched protest while I clipped the remaining nails. I planned to tell the story to Frank, and I left.

A surrogate child, I stood at his bed. There were things I wanted to tell him—more than the toenail story—but I slipped my hand into his and waited. He moved his lips, but his breath emerged without any words.

"Rest," I said. "Let me do the talking for once."

He twisted his face in frustration and tried again. "You and me," he said.

"Yes, I'm here." He shook his head, his frustration growing, and now I understood. "With the dogs?" I asked. "You mean partners?"

He nodded and closed his eyes, his face in repose.

The nurse hurried in. "Too much excitement," she said. "You have to get out."

"No more," I said. "We'll be quiet." But she insisted, and because I thought my going would help him, I left.

I waited in the lounge. I saw some ambulance attendants bring another patient, his eyes wide with fear, while his family, distracted by the strange surroundings, looked everywhere but at him. Later, I sat with Frank while he slept, and much later I dozed in a chair in the lounge.

It must be late. There's no one left in the lounge, and hardly anybody's in the corridor. Eleven-ten. I'm startled, fully

awake. At the door to Coronary Care there are two orderlies, one of them holding the door for the other who's
pushing a gurney. I stand up and follow, and they take the
gurney to the room I know is Frank's. I return to my chair.
Maybe he's only going to X-Ray.

They're back. I was afraid the guardrails would be up
and a sheet would be draped across them, but the gurney's
just as it was, with no one on it, with that silly-looking
cover, like a skimpy bed-skirt, hanging half-way down.

Suddenly I know what kind of gurney it is.

The orderlies are taking him away, and I am not ready
to see him go. I call out to them, and run, and grab the
edge of the gurney.

"I don't know where he'll be buried," I say to the man,
"maybe back east—and I want to see him, just for a minute."

One of the orderlies searches my eyes. "No, I don't think
I can, Miss. You better ask at the desk."

I turn to the other one, who looks about in the hall and
shrugs. "Why don't you just let her?" he asks.

I slip the flimsy cover from under his hands, and, as if
this were some puzzle, there's another cover, shaped like
the first one, but green, made of rubber. I slowly remove a
corner of it, and Frank is there in a metal pan—like a
butcher-shop pan, but man-size—with sides, as if to prevent his juices from spilling. But I'm at the wrong end of
the gurney. Through the framework of wire that supports
the covers, I can see the shape of feet underneath the plastic shroud. I replace the covers here and uncover the other
end of the gurney.

I pull the upper part of the shroud away from his face.
No one had to close his eyes for him, I'm sure—he looks

exactly as he did when I said "Partners?" And not much different from the day he said I should have fought. Like all too much of what I have learned, I learned it late, as if because of lethargy, or of reluctance to live, I had willed away the simple truths.

If Frank could tell me, what would he want of me now?

Though I haven't prayed in years, nor even believe in prayer, instinct tells me that prayer—despite all that happened to him—is what Frank would want. Or am I looking for something, anything, to do for him, and therefore for me.

I bend toward him and, with two of my fingers, trace a scar on his jaw near the tip of his ear. I try to tame his eyebrows into tidy, even lines, but the hairs, like silver wires, resist me. Words resist me as well, and those that come at last I offer silently, on his behalf, and trust that if Frank had heard them, he'd have found them good.

Two Women, One Child

Can it be that I will give my granddaughter back her child? And without putting up a fight? She arrived only minutes ago with a young man I've never seen and—like borrowing an egg—said, "We've come for Rachel."

I couldn't understand why she would visit on a Monday.

"I sent you a letter," she said, "didn't you get it? She still doesn't *know?*"

What Shelley meant was suddenly clear, but I—as if I could keep it from happening—answered, "Right this *minute* you'll take her?"

And she, defensive, said, "I told you I wrote!"

The young man touched her arm—a gentle placating touch. She shook her head in frustration, and when she said his name, he offered his hand as uncertainly as if he thought I wouldn't take it. He is oriental. Did he think I'd reject him for that? Does he know as little of me as I of him?

Rachel, who seconds before had hugged him, was reading my eyes, as she had on a terrible day three years ago, when she was less than two, when Shelley had arrived with a different young man—then too without having given a hint in advance. I hadn't liked the look of that one—patronising, put-upon—and when I'd protested against their taking Rachel, Shelley had said, "Don't be bitchy, Gram. You're making her nervous."

Rachel had not seemed nervous to me, neither then nor two weeks later when Shelley, convinced she wasn't ready to keep her, returned her to me. Nor, though she seemed a bit solemn, was she nervous today.

Still, to make sure I hadn't alarmed her, I said, "Mendocino isn't far, darling. You'll come to me here, and I'll go to you there." To Shelley I said, "She has to have lunch," and to Rachel again, "Let's have a lamb chop and corn."

Rachel cocked her head in surprise—meat is normally dinner—but quickly she turned to Shelley and Michael and offered to help them pack.

I am now in the kitchen alone, indecisive, ineffectual, dimly hearing them talk but unable to hear about what. I start to prepare some salad, and Shelley comes in, forlorn, and leans against the wall.

"Gram?" I glance at her. "This time," she says, "I'll be able to keep her." I have nothing to say in answer. "Gram? Until I got into high school, you talked to me the way you talk to Rachel. With love in your voice."

"I don't know what you're talking about," I say. "I always talk to you nicely, and I. . . ."

She slams her hand on the wall. "Exactly! Nicely! You're

polite! And even that much is only for Rachel's sake."

As if I hadn't heard her, I say, "And I was being friendly to Michael too, wasn't I? I don't know what you want." I shake my head in a clearly dismissive way, but I know exactly what she means, and what she has said is true.

She turns and, as she leaves me, says, "It's hopeless. You'll never forget that day at the counselor's office."

As if that day—which we have never discussed—were the start or the end of our problems. What happened then was that Shelley told a counselor her mother had said she should give the baby away for adoption, but that she had decided to keep it—except, she said with a shrug, after her mother died, and after the baby was born, she didn't want it, and here was her grandmother now, hassling her not to give it away.

With a deliberate forefinger, the counselor settled his hair back of his ears. He consulted his sandals and socks and said, "An adult's main business in life is to become his own person. Shelley is an adult. Therefore."

Shelley said that that was it! She couldn't become her own person if she had to belong to the baby. I had heard about 'own person' before, but the counselor told me to listen. I did, and when I said, "What about the baby? Where does this thinking lead? Why is it always right?", he told me that counselors didn't presume to judge.

Near the kitchen door, Michael, holding a carton, says softly, "Cut it out, Shel, *I'll* carry. *You* have to stay here and talk."

He leaves, and Shelley, somewhat resentful, enters the kitchen again. Indeed for Rachel's sake, I have to establish a truce, and I am about to say that Michael seems nice, when Shelley recites, "He's twenty-six and has a degree in

Bio from Berkeley. I've known him eight months, and the store I work at?—he owns it."

"I'm impressed," I say, and I mean it, but as I hear the words, I'm sure they sound sarcastic. "Besides," I add, "Rachel said he's nice." Despite my intentions, my own resentment flares, and I ask, "But why did I learn about him from Rachel? All these months he's been coming here with you—why didn't you ever bring him in so we could meet?"

"And why are you thinking about your pride? Isn't this better for Rachel?"

Maybe it is, and maybe I ought to admit it, but before I can answer at all, she again turns and leaves, and now, though I've shown but a shred of my anger, I regret what I've said. I'm afraid she'll vent her resentment on Rachel. I believe, in fact, that Shelley has not forgiven *me* for the day we saw the counselor any more than I have forgiven her. That day, I said that if she indeed was giving the baby away, I wanted the baby myself.

"You're sixty-five," she answered. "You'll be dead before she grows up."

"My grandmother lived till ninety," I said. "With luck, I'll survive till your child has her own illegitimate child."

Shelley's eyes narrowed, and I knew then as now that she, not I, had the power to choose what to do with her child, and that sarcasm and tit-for-tat cruelty were worse than useless in trying to move her. I therefore made her an offer: in place of an inheritance in the nebulous future, five thousand dollars right then, to use however she chose, toward becoming her own person. Shelley said it wasn't because of the offer of money—she could see some real advantages to Rachel—and she accepted.

In effect, I had bought her month-old child, not because I already loved Rachel—I didn't—but because I was the one who could take her. Had my own Rachel—Shelley's mother—lived, she, perhaps, would have done so, but it's something of which I cannot be sure. Nor do I know if I will ever be free of thinking my daughter might not have sickened and died if Shelley hadn't been in all that trouble that she summarizes in "when I got into high school." I wish the studies suggesting a link between stress and cancer had never been done.

Michael returns from the car and says, "I hope you won't worry about Rachel."

"In fact I will, Michael," I say, "but not because of you. I trust you."

I had stressed the word "trust," but he, as if I had stressed "you," answers, "It's time you trusted Shelley too."

I bristle against the charge of unfairness implied. I want to ask him why I should trust her, why *he* trusts her.

Instead, I ask, "Would you join Rachel for lunch?"

"Thank you, no. Just Rachel will be fine."

"Then will you please send her in?"

She comes in with an armload of books. She's decided to leave them, so that when she comes to visit I'll have them on hand for reading to her. Practical Rachel, pre-M.B.A.

She takes her knife and fork and carefully cuts her meat by herself. This is a matter of honor with her, and she doesn't even glance toward me for approval. I watch, hoping she'll look up, and at last she does and returns my smile. She shrugs modestly. Suddenly I know this day is real, and I am overwhelmed with loss. I have to give Shelley her child, and this time she'll keep her, and Rachel doesn't mind.

She has known Shelley almost four years. She knows that Shelley is her mother, but despite what she has seen of families in books, she doesn't seem to consider it strange that she's living with me. At the playground, more of the children are there with sitters than with mothers, and I wonder if living with any female adult is all she expects.

"Is it a surprise," I ask, "that you're going to live with Mommy?" She nods. "You always have *fun* with Mommy," I add. Again she nods in agreement.

And why not? I—though I'm healthy and strong and expect to live till Rachel is grown—am not fun. I can no longer make a child shriek with delight. I'm sure I never made my own Rachel shriek with delight. During years of poverty, when my children were young, even laughter was scarce in our home. The failure was mine, and it is my deepest regret. But, oh, what antics I used to perform for Shelley. I was wiser by then, and secure, and those I loved all were alive.

I don't believe, in fact, that even when Shelley was well into high school my love for her was gone from my voice. What I felt for her then was sorrow—for her neglected talents, for truancy, for who-knew-what adventures with unsavory-looking friends—so if I felt this sorrow, how could there not have been love in my voice? Or perhaps her perception is right.

"Gram?" Rachel is solemn. "Who will you play with?" she asks. "Will you go back to the campus?"

Her question shocks me. It implies some knowledge I didn't know she had. The university is right nearby, and countless times I've taken her there. We've walked beside the palms and oak and eucalyptus and gathered seed-pods sculpted like stars. We've talked of why the hills turn green

in the winter, gold in the spring, and listened to the lan-
guages of foreign students—but none of this is what Rachel
means.

"Mommy says you'll go, but Michael says you're too
old."

"When did they say all this?"

"Just now. Gram, are you old?"

"I don't know, dear. Give me a minute to think."

What does Michael know about old? And what does
Shelley know about the campus? She thought my love for
it was a joke.

Rachel takes her plate to the sink, giving me the time I
asked her for. I want to hold her, or at least to touch her
hair, but I'm afraid she'll sense too much. She returns and
nibbles her grapes.

"Mommy says you used to go to lectures there, but you
didn't pay, so you weren't really supposed to go."

"That was dishonest, yes."

I wait to hear what else her mommy has told her I did,
but after a second or two she turns to one of her books
and reads to herself, from memory.

Old. What kinds of old, or of passion, do they know
about? Do they know that a woman of sixty, widowed,
with no education to speak of, could wander onto a campus and find—seize—a goal for what's left of her life? I
bought the finest leather handbag I'd ever owned, and two
wool suits, and for five years I walked among the throngs
of students to the lecture halls, as if I belonged there, as if
I were a faculty wife entitled to audit the classes, as if I had
met my husband at a Harvard-Wellesley Mixer instead of
at the factory nearby—for five years listened and read as
fiercely as if indeed I could make up for the previous fifty.

Shelley would no doubt think it "gross," or at least hilarious, to know that I had fantasized remarriage then with a certain handsome professor. It was early in the first year, in the only philosophy class I could find that was not only easy but large enough to keep me from giving myself away by getting too friendly and talking too much. He had answered a question, and then he had added, "But I say that descriptively, and not pejoratively." Some magic in that sentence so exhilarated me that afterward I left the path I normally took and, self-consciously, certain that no professor's wife would ever be caught in so childish an act, I circled a eucalyptus tree again and again, my hand on its trunk, stroking it where it was pale and smooth, and sniffed its bark that hung in strips, and gathered its slender leaves in my bag, hearing, "descriptively and not pejoratively." Later, when I repeated the words to Shelley, she laughed. I did not laugh when I gave up the campus to raise her child.

"*Are* you old?" Rachel asks.

"No. I really don't think so."

Michael is in the doorway how. "Rachel, we're packed. Want to come to the station for gas?"

She goes with him gladly, and the house is suddenly quiet. Why is Shelley still in the bedroom if all they are taking is packed? And why, since Shelley is doing what long ago I said she should do, can't *I* go in there and ask?

Her step is suddenly loud in the carpeted hall, and she is in front of me, facing me squarely, sitting in the chair where minutes ago Rachel had sat. Her voice is quiet, controlled.

"Beginning today, I'm your equal. I live a life as competent as anybody else's, but as soon as I walk through your door I'm a child. Either I whine, or I lash out. Never again."

There is a note of assurance, indeed of maturity, in her tone, but some inner voice cautions me not to believe her.

"Do *I* make you act like a child?"

"No, I'm to blame for that, but *you* take advantage of it when I do. The weaker I act, the stronger you become."

"Then you've learned something useful, Shelley, but what is it you want of me?"

"I'm not asking anything of you. It's only when you're weak that you have to ask."

Her words frighten me. I can imagine never seeing Rachel again if Shelley should so decide.

"Did you think?" she asks, "that I'd leave here with Rachel without even telling you, 'thanks?' "

I want to ask why not—when in the last five years have I heard her say "thanks"? Though I am silent, my silence is answer enough, and she shakes her head in disgust.

"I'm sorry you'll have to be lonely," she says, "but later you'll see I've done you a favor."

"Is that why you're taking her—to do me a favor? Don't do me the favor."

"That almost sounds funny," she says. "Still. You've plenty to do to keep yourself busy. You used to keep busy by running around on the campus."

I could kill her.

"What's the matter?" she asks, "What did I do now?"

I can't prevent the welling up of tears, but I manage to keep them from falling. Her head moves forward, as if from a little bit closer she'll fathom why there are tears.

"All right," she says. "Maybe you aren't interested in lectures any more—I wasn't telling you what to do—there's *lots* around here for seniors to do." I feel my color continue to rise. "Can I get us some coffee?" she asks.

Despite my silence—indeed, I suspect, to escape it—she stands and goes to the stove. I dab at my eyes. I can't afford to let her be angry at me. She places a cup of coffee before me, appraises me and sits at the table again.

"Michael will keep her out for a while to give us some time. They'll go for gas and ice cream and maybe a walk. I want to know," she says, "why you got angry a minute ago." I don't answer, and she repeats, "I want to know."

My fear quickens. "And if I don't do as you say, you won't allow me to visit your child?"

Evenly and slowly she says, "I'll always allow you to visit my child." She searches my eyes and surely sees my relief. "Despite how you've acted toward me," she adds, "I know that you'd never be mean to Rachel."

"I see. To you I was mean. Would you go so far as to say that for whatever I did that was mean you've now forgiven me?"

"It's when you're weak that you have to forgive. It was when I was dependent that I forgave you."

"And now that you're no longer dependent?"

"I'm not sure. But I want to know if you're angry at me for taking Rachel."

This is a simpler question to answer than why I am angry. Carefully, I say, "I'm not angry at you for taking her. You're the one she belongs with."

Her shoulders droop with relief. Her mother is dead since a month before Rachel was born, and I, I suppose, have taken her place. She squares her shoulders.

"So were the tears because of losing her?"

"Shelley, what does it matter? It's better for her to find us discussing what she'll be needing for school."

"It matters to *me*. I'm getting my child, but it isn't enough.

I *am* still angry, and so are you."

"What did *you* have to be angry about? What did *I* ever do to *you?*"

"I tried to tell you before! You became so polite! You never asked a personal question, as if it wouldn't be proper, as if I were a stranger, as if the answer didn't affect you."

"Because when I asked, you resented my asking."

"So you paid me back by resenting my resentment even *after* I started to change. You stopped looking at me. Till I gave you Rachel you battled me—afterward, nothing. You didn't even criticize when I abandoned her the second time, never asked me why, as if it was just what you'd expected— I was irresponsible. And that scheme you dreamed up— that money you offered that made me so cheap."

"But you said I'd be dead before she grew up. If I hadn't offered the money you'd have given her over to strangers."

"If you'd said, 'So when I die, *then* you can give her away,' I'd have said you could have her. But no, you made that 'illegitimate child' remark. And later, when I started coming to see her, you acted so neighborly, as if I were some childless old woman you were giving a treat to, a chance to play with a baby. Asking nothing of me, letting me play and go away guilty, knowing that *you* were left with the *shit.*"

I feel that word like a blow to the head. "Damn you, Shelley, *damn* you. *I* gave up what you *dare* to describe as 'running around on the campus.' To keep myself *busy* you call it? *Now* you'll be responsible? *Now* you love your child? Your mother was *my* child."

Her face goes white. Though I had surmised a bit of what she has revealed, I have said what I vowed I never would say—what I have left unsaid even when I have hated

Shelley most—and I have said it on the day she has claimed her child. And all because of that ugly word she constantly used in those terrible years, that in recent months she no longer has used, and that I cannot abide even today when everyone else I know has already adjusted to it. And yet my rage, unleashed, has given me strength. Now indeed I believe we are equals. I know what I have done, and I don't know whether I'm sorry or glad.

The color slowly returns to her face. She is strikingly calm, and her eyes are averted from mine. When at last she answers, she says, "Even before they did that study on stress as maybe triggering cancer, I thought I had made my mother die. I was afraid if I knew for sure how a woman feels about her child, I'd know I really had. So I was afraid to love Rachel. All that time I wanted you to tell me, 'Shelley, it wasn't your fault.' " She pauses. "It was Michael who said you couldn't release me from this, because you can't really know. That it's something I have to live with. People die before you can explain, and before *they* can explain." She suddenly turns her eyes to mine, and after a moment or two, averts them again and strokes the sides of her cup. "How I love Michael," she says.

When she was thirteen, or even twelve, she was always in love and always told me, but never since then. I recognize what she has offered me, but for me it's too soon to respond.

"I knew you blamed me," she says, "but hearing it still is a shock." Suddenly she shakes her head in apparent amazement. "But I never suspected that *that* was smoldering too—that you were so angry at not being able to go to the lectures."

She lowers her eyes, and I think she's trying to say that

she's sorry. I believe that whether I'm fully ready or not, it's time I said it as well, but these and other simple words that only a dozen years ago would have sprung to my lips, by now are trapped inside me, sunk by their own weight. I move my hand toward hers, and though she doesn't fully withdraw, she squares her shoulders again and thereby seems to distance herself. I take my cue and do nothing more.

"She doesn't have enough jeans for school," she says.

"Rachel? No. I was waiting for the last minute. They grow so fast. And it's cold and damp in Mendocino—she'll need a heavier parka. Is there time to go shopping today?"

"There's really no rush—I can get it up there."

"Will you have enough money?"

"Oh yes. The store's a raging success."

She looks at her hands. Her skin is clear, with the healthy color it had when she was a child, and her hair is beautifully cut. I remember a day on the campus when Rachel and I stood at a gully after a rainy week. Rachel had taken a twig from the stream and turned to show it just as a student rode by on her bike—a girl with hair that was dark and long, as Shelley's then was long, and Rachel exclaimed, "Mommy!" and saw her mistake.

I turn my face toward the window, afraid she'll look up. I know there is more we should say to each other before she must leave, but I have been drained of resources. If Michael would only come in he'd rescue us both.

"I think you should go when they get back," I say. "If you wait, she'll nap in the car and then be awake at night."

"When will you come to visit?" she asks. I shrug. "Next week?" she asks. Without turning, I nod. "Would you like to move to Mendocino?" she asks.

I'm startled—gratified—by her offer and meet her gaze.

"I think not, Shelley. That wouldn't be best, would it?—four hours drive isn't far."

She nods in agreement and once again examines her hands. The discussion is closed.

I gauge her weight and the width of her shoulders. "I'll knit a new sweater," I say.

"But a bigger one, for later on," she says. "She has more than enough for now."

"For you." She does not appear to understand. "A heavy one?" I ask, and then in a rush, "For *you*, Shelley, can you use a heavy one?"

She becomes nonplussed. "Oh. I guess."

"A heavy pullover, right?"

Still hesitant, she nods. "Would . . . ? Could you maybe make me a blue one?"

"Light blue?" I ask her. "Navy? Which blue?"

"Surprise me," she says.

Present Tense

My mother searches for misery and, when she finds it, accuses me of bringing it. Today, as if her suspicion were fact, she informs me, "It wasn't us you came to see. You came for Broadway shows."

She weights perhaps eighty pounds, and her pallor is ghastly. I don't know what to say about her appearance, and choose to respond to her words instead. As if her statement were merely an honest mistake, I answer, "If that were the case, I'd have come for a weekend—not for a week. I have tickets for two shows."

"You'll sleep in a hotel and eat in restaurants. My house isn't clean enough for you."

"Is that what you think?"

In the past I would have protested at length, explained, reassured her, or tried to, but now that my answer is only a question, she is diverted, blocked from her old routine.

She takes a roll, bites into it and leans against the kitchen sink, chewing. I move to the table, to the chair from which I can see her best, and she says, "What difference does it make what I think? All that matters is that *you're* happy."

She has said this before, many times, and I have waited, wondering if, when she offered this burden of guilt again, I would be strong enough to turn it away. The moment has come, and I feel invulnerable. In the glow of my self-approval, I become more generous toward her as well. I'm tempted to go to her and push a stray white wisp upward and under her hairnet, but I'm not tempted quite enough. When I embraced her minutes ago, her response was cold.

"When I phoned to tell you the date I would come, you said it's a lot of work for you, remember?" I wait for her answer, and the answer doesn't come in words, but rather in a subtle relaxation of the muscles in her face and shoulders. Her mouth, which was firm only seconds ago, droops a bit, completing a portrait of grief. "Instead of wasting time in extra work," I add, "we'll go out a lot and walk in the sun."

She recovers. Decisively she says, "I don't go in the sun. The sun bleaches."

The last three words are an axiom—I can tell by her tone. She instructs me with this axiom, as she has done with others in a list which includes

Girls who wear glasses are ugly.

Doctors don't know anything.

Only a sister is a true friend.

She has never had sisters. She has had two children, however, one of whom died at forty-nine. On the day of his funeral, she said of me, "She is my life." That was ten years ago, when I was forty-five.

"Remember Sonny's hair?" she asks, "how bleached it was from the sun?" She lowers her head a bit, recalling my brother. "I remember when he was three," she says. Suddenly she is transformed, animated, laughing. "We were in the country then, at Miller's place." She retells the story in all its detail, just as she told it when I was a child. Its essence is that Sonny disappeared on a Friday in summer, and the women searched the farmhouse, sent for Miller, did what he told them, ran to look in the fields and woods, while Sonny reached the road, walked to the village, waited for and met the train on which the husbands all arrived on weekends. *"No* one had a child as smart as Sonny was."

Suddenly she thinks of something else, perhaps that he is dead, or more likely that all his life he did what he wanted. By the time he'd reached his teens, his cleverness had lost its charm—for her. She turns to the window, her face in profile. Her head is thrust forward, and her lips are moving rapidly, without a sound.

My father says nothing. He is eating, and he does not talk when he eats. He concentrates hard on his food. He's sleek, and he looks no more than sixty-five.

Watching him, I wonder once again if there is any point in trying to talk about their way of life, which, in the year since my last visit, I have, by turns, analyzed to shreds or thrust from my mind.

I want to talk about the way they eat their meals. My mother carries my father's food across the large rectangular kitchen to the table and then returns to the sink to eat her own food, standing up. It has always been this way, and when I was a child I thought this was normal. I can guess how this practise got started, of course, but she has been in America since she was twelve, and before she dies I want her to discover she is her husband's equal. I turn to speak to her of it, but she has become so old this year that I'm afraid if she learns it now it will hurt her more than help her.

"I remember Miller's place, Mama. It had a creek with trees along its banks, and a wonderful meadow with yellow flowers. And the water came from a well and was cold and sweet, like no other water I've tasted since."

My words are effective, and she nods. "It was in Ellenville," she says.

"It was in Yaegerville," my father says.

"In Yaegerville," she repeats, annoyed. "There were only two beds in Yaegerville, so where did she sleep?"

"You're absolutely right," he answers. "In Yaegerville there were only two beds. One for us and one for Sonny. It was the *second* time we went to Miller's, five years later, that he had the place she remembers. But where Sonny came to the station to meet me was in Yaegerville."

She does not see at once that she was right, that in Ellenville indeed was the place I had described, and before I can point this out, she turns on me, again her betrayer. "Did you also bring your own jar of instant coffee?"

"No, when I want coffee I'll use some of yours, okay?"

She eats her roll fiercely. I am being hard on her, and I know it. I have changed the rules of the game without consulting her. She has a repertory of rehearsed retorts to all the things she has fantasized I will say, and I am saying none of them. She is searching for a way to misconstrue my latest remark, groping, in fact, for a way, as indeed she must grope for physical things, because my mother is blind.

She does not admit it, however. She has only recently, now that her vision is irrevocably gone, admitted to having "a condition."

"I'm ready for my apple," my father calls out. He always has an apple at lunch, because he's convinced what they say about apples and doctors is true. This is not to say he avoids doctors. He basks in their attention, in their admiration of how fit he is, and the difference between my parents' views of doctors gives them something to argue about when there isn't another subject at hand.

My mother touches the wall with her left hand, turns a bit to the right and slowly comes to the table, bringing the apple. She holds it out to my father with her right hand, he puts the empty dinnerplate into her left one, and she returns to the sink hesitantly, without the self-assurance of those who have confronted the fact of their blindness, acknowledged it, and tried to learn some ways to cope with it. Her myopia progressed for almost seventy years in some process not yet understood, and her retinas at last disintegrated, and she, except beside her stove and kitchen sink, is like a woman struck blind an hour ago.

My father tests the temperature of the apple with the palms of both his hands and judges the apple to be too cold. Warming it in his hands, he begins to unfold the chronicle of a year of visits to his doctor, frequent checkups, "just to make sure." I have read it all in his letters and heard it all on the phone, but I resign myself to listening, and I merely glance at my mother, who is washing his dishes.

She lifts the roll from the drainboard, daintily, with wet thumb and forefinger, and takes another bite, and only now do I become aware that she has had nothing but that for her lunch. I am catapulted back to the early thirties. My father, my brother and I had chicken, vegetables, milk, fruit. There were even pennies available for Hershey bars and charlotte russes in the winter and ice cream pops in summer, because heavy cream and chocolate were healthy, my mother told us, for growing children. But my mother ate only bread, and when I asked her why, she said, "Wait till you're a mother. Then you'll understand." Later, when my father was working again, although it was years before I could see the events were connected, she added some cheese to her diet, and finally chicken and vegetables too.

I now suspect inflation has taken her back to her diet of bread. Appalled, I stare at my father, who is giving me a word-for-word restatement of the doctor's latest praise. I interrupt. "How does the doctor explain why Mama's become so thin?"

"How can he explain? She doesn't let him do tests."

"Tests," she says with contempt. "Excuses to steal your money. He asks questions, but I don't answer him. If he's so smart, let *him* figure out what's wrong with me."

"Why did you go to him?" I ask.

"I fainted. He gave me medicines, samples, but I threw them away. And I didn't faint again anyway." She lifts her head a little in pride. She has outwitted the doctor.

My father returns to his story in all its detail. I am increasingly agitated, but he doesn't seem to notice. Soon he pats the apple against his cheek, decides the apple is tepid enough to be eaten and postpones the narration, while my mother, still at the sink, starts on a slice of bread.

I can no longer restrain myself. "Why are you eating so much bread?"

"I'm not even allowed to eat bread?"

"I mean why are you eating *nothing* but bread?"

Her mouth twitches in a quickly aborted smile, and though I see at once that I have blundered into her trap, it is too late to escape. "So what?" she asks innocently. "It's whole wheat bread."

"You *know* that isn't enough. No *wonder* you're so thin."

As I thrash about in the trap, she lets herself smile. "Do you want to show how devoted you are? Move back to New York."

There.

I committed the offense almost twenty years ago. She reminds me of it again, but now with a smile, and it is this that tells me there is no forgiveness.

That day, when I broke the news to her, she was devastated. "California? You can't."

"I can't put it off any more. Nowadays careers. . . ."

"You can't. I don't want to know about careers. Who will I go to on weekends? Who will I talk to?"

"You can move there too."

"Papa leave his friends? He would *never* do it."

"But I can't keep refusing my husband because of my father's friends."

"*Make* Paul stay." And finally the words I could hardly believe I had heard: "You *hate* me. I gave you everything, and you took it, and now you're going to leave me."

And now, as she waits for my answer again, I see no use in telling her that I will not move back. I turn to my father. "Is she eating nothing but bread today because *I'm* here, or does she *always* do that now?"

He turns around in his chair for a second to glance toward the sink, in the way he would turn if someone had entered the room and he had to know who. He shrugs. "How should

I know what she eats? I don't give her orders about what to eat."

"I *know* that. But you go shopping with her. Or you go without her. Are you buying for one or for two?"

"Anne, darling. I'm not a housewife. I don't figure out portions. She tells me a list, I buy what she wants, I pay, I eat what she puts in front of me, and I don't spy on her."

"I'm going for a walk," I say, rising.

"You just got off the plane. You didn't even go to your hotel," he says. "Rest awhile, sweetie."

"I need the walk." I wish I had, in fact, gone to my hotel. I turn to the sink, and my mother is still smiling.

I hurry along the streets for a while without any plan. When I was young and pregnant, it seemed that wherever I looked there were pregnant women, and today it seems that whoever I see is old or as old as I. I change direction. On the avenue there are stores, and there will surely be children.

There, I slow my pace almost at once. I'm attracted soon to a little store, old and strangely appealing. It's an optician's shop, but it's not like the ones I'm accustomed to now, with their rows upon rows of designer frames in purple and glitter, plastic and wire.

Here, an elderly man is at work, and between his workbench and the window is a plain display: a drawing of an eye and, in front of it, four pairs of glasses. They are not empty frames, but glasses, and they look like the man might have saved them here since the days when he learned his trade. They're like the ones I saw as a child, when I used to stand at the optician's window, gravely, examining the glasses with respect and loathing. Girls who wear glasses are ugly.

One of the pairs of glasses here has a tortoise-shell frame. When I was seven, and it was clear to everyone that I needed glasses, and still my mother refused, my teacher, in an imperious note, summoned my mother to school and over-ruled her. The glasses I got had a tortoise-shell frame, and they became my perfect eyes and my deformity.

None of the glasses here is rimless, like the ones I wore on the day of my wedding. Then, as I reached the carpeted aisle, my father—to prevent my mother from making a scene—quickly, smoothly, without any warning, removed my glasses and handed them off to my brother.

These could have been my mother's. They would have saved her countless falls, occasional broken bones and the terror of two children who never knew when she would next be hurt. One of the four, in fact, is—in shape, but by no means in thickness—like the ones she finally got when she had to. On Sonny's thirty-seventh birthday, she left the menswear shop with a scarlet sweater and tripped on a German shepherd asleep in the sun, and Sonny's fury, when he later saw her injuries, forced my father, at last, to inter-vene.

I don't know how many minutes have passed, but I see that the elderly man is staring at me. He is no doubt won-dering why anyone would think his small display is worth the scrutiny that I have given it. I, however, have never told anyone what glasses as homely as these could have done when my mother was young and could still have been helped by them.

I slowly leave the window and go to the corner, looking

for something to do that's better than aimlessly walking about. I cross the street to the delicatessen. I am convinced that if I bring some corned beef back with me, my mother, despite the previous games, will agree to eat it, and we will spend a peaceful afternoon that she will remember with pleasure.

When I return, I stand in the hall outside my parents' apartment door. They are bickering again, because she has just discovered he made a mistake. She wanted "jumbo" eggs, and what he bought this morning were only "large." I listen awhile, but my interest is almost clinical, and I wonder, as I have wondered before, whether when they die I will be grieved, and again I hope I will, because to be otherwise still seems inhuman.

I knock on the door, and the argument stops. My father, muttering about eggs, lets me in but avoids my eyes. I cross the length of the room to the kitchen table, and my mother says, "So soon back already?"

"I did what I went to do. I took a walk, and I went to the delicatessen."

I tear the outer bag noisily and turn it into a surface on which to divide the salads and meats. My father approaches. "Corned beef? I already ate lunch."

"I know you did. This is for Mama and me. I'll get more for us all tomorrow, okay? There's nothing like the corned beef you get in New York. Or the sauerkraut either. Smell it. I also got paper plates and plastic forks, so we can have a picnic and then have nothing to wash."

And now for the first time since I have reentered the kitchen, I turn to look at my mother. Her face is alert and peaceful. She moves away from the sink, resolutely, neglecting to feel for the wall. The angle at which she approaches the table is wrong, and she is walking far too fast. "Mama!" I shout, but her slippered foot goes forward, and as it strikes the edge of the suitcase and her body topples, the palms of my hands fly up to my eyes, and I'm twelve again, and she's hurtling down the stairs of the theater balcony, and a crowd has formed, and I can't get close to see if she's moving, but I finally hear the familiar excuse: "That's what I get for talking instead of looking where I'm walking." Some of the people move on, but others are in the aisle or sitting beside it, and again I do what I'm not allowed to do: I take her elbow as she starts to climb the stairs. And she—as she has done countless times—swings the elbow hard against my ribs and whispers, "Ssssssstop it!"

I am now beside her. She is eighty-one and on her knees, and with her fingers she rests on the rim of my suitcase.

"I'm so sorry, Mama. I thought it was out of your way. Are you hurt?"

I'm afraid to move her or even to touch her. I examine the way that one of her legs is turned at an angle beneath her, and I calculate how best to lift her.

"Hurt?" she asks. "Who cares if I'm hurt?"

"Try to stand. I'm going to lift you to your feet, but if you're in any pain at all, say so quick." I tell my father to bring her a chair.

I lift her slowly and try to ease her into the chair, but she resists me. "Don't tell me to sit! I don't want to sit." She plants her feet on the floor, rigidly, while my hands are still on her ribs. She tests her balance, shifting her weight from one of her legs to the other.

"Try to take a step," I say. She takes two, turns and

takes two more. "Sit down and rest a minute," I say, moving a hand to her elbow.

At once she is herself again, her younger, stronger self, and she jabs me viciously. "Ssssstop it!" she says. "I don't *need* you."

I have backed away. She is about five feet away from me, staring, and her eyes, if she could see, would be focused below my chin. Her face is white, rigid, and her lips are pressed together so hard they have all but disappeared. She folds her arms across her chest and waits.

My father takes a newspaper out of a stack of a dozen or more on a table beside a reclinable chair. He sits down in the chair, and he's reading.

I lunge at the little table, raise the stack of papers as high as my shoulders and fling the stack to the floor. On the shelf of the table there is a wrought-iron bowl. I snatch it up and hurl it across the room at the stove as hard as I can.

My father stands up, stupefied, gaping.

My mother's hands go up to protect her face, and her head jerks left to down to right to left, following terrible sounds. "What *is* it?" she cries, "what *is* it?"

"It's *me!*" I shout. *"Throwing* things."

My mother lowers her hands, hesitantly, first one a little and then the other. She is bewildered. "You? Throwing? Since when do you throw?"

"Since now!"

She considers my answer. "But why?"

"Figure it *out*. You're so *smart.*"

She is motionless, speechless.

My father bends to the floor and starts to restack the papers. He glances repeatedly at me, measuring my rage.

He leaves the stack on the floor and goes to retrieve the bowl.

My mother has not moved.

I walk to the suitcase and lift it. I put it back on the floor and drag it instead. I drag it across the room and push it under the table, where it should have been all along, and I turn to look at my mother.

She has followed the sounds, and her eyes are on me. Her face is composed. Again she fold her arms across her chest. She has drawn her conclusions, and now in a tiny gesture, a firming of lips, she informs me she's saving her thoughts for some future remark.

We are silent. Nor could we move toward one another if we were commanded to. We are past explanation or apology. We are separate at last, and we are inseparable after all.

Part Two

My Father
and
Signor Corelli

In 1943, food was scarce in Rome, but worse—for my father— was the scarcity of cigarettes. He would rise before dawn, cross the city and stand in line at a tobacconist's, and I, entranced by the very idea of being awake when most of the world was asleep, begged him to once—on my birthday—take me along. It was the sixteenth of October, when I was twelve.

We stood in line in the rain, conspirators against my mother who was at home, warm in bed and convinced, we were sure, that I would be catching a cold. Afterward, we made our way again across the city, and when we reached the building where we lived, we found that our apartment door was sealed, and that all of the Jews, including my mother and sister, had been taken away.

I don't believe my father had any idea whatever of where he was going that day. We merely fled, dodging around the corners when we saw on the streets in front of us the German trucks. I say "I don't believe," because we never discussed it. There are Jews I know who could speak of their losses at once, and others who broke their silence only when decades had passed. My father, however, never did. Once a year we would light memorial candles, one for my mother and another for my sister. Except for that single display of remembrance, we acted as if, on that peculiar autumn day, he and I had sprung from the earth together, father and daughter, complete.

It was in that haphazard flight across the city that we found Signor Corelli. A tramway system office opened onto the street, and through its window we saw him—a short man with a useless arm and a lame leg—crossing the room to a desk.

My father, choking with grief and exertion, pleaded, "Signore, hide us—the Germans are searching for Jews."

Where could he send us, he answered, how did he know that wherever he sent us we would be safe? And since there wasn't an answer to that, he said, "You'd better come home with me."

At his home they talked, asked about each other's families and work, but my father was still distraught when Emilio, Signor Corelli's son, stood in the doorway hours afterward, home from his job.

Incredulous—hearing his father's account of why we were there—he said, "Papà! Why must you keep them? Didn't the Germans beat you enough?"

My father's glance shot to Signor Corelli. Pointing to the crippled leg, he asked, "Signore?"

"No, no," he said with a wave of his hand. "1917. Wounds from the *other* war."

Emilio turned to my father. "He argued for one of his men with one of their officers, here, in Rome. They beat him, sent him back to me swollen and bloody. What about *him?*"

My father sat down, his elbows on his knees, the palms of his hands supporting his head.

"Emilio," Signor Corelli said. "You will address him as 'Professore.' They are staying. *You* can go to the village, to your mother and the little ones."

But Emilio stayed. He was eighteen. To my childish eyes he was very tall, and even by my father's standards he was handsome. The way he touched his father's arm—gently— moved us both, and I longed for Emilio's love.

We lived together, the Corellis in one of the bedrooms, my father and I in the other. Soap with which to be doing the laundry was scarce, so to limit the number of sheets we would use, I slept with my father, and Emilio with his.

Several times during those months, Signor Corelli cried out in his sleep, and my father leapt from our bed, to return in a minute and say the signore had only been dreaming, Emilio knew how to talk to him, go back to sleep, everything's fine. But for days after each of his father's nightmares, Emilio hardly looked at my father or me, confirming that because of us his father was living in fear.

Till January fourth. There was a knock at the door, and my father and I, from our bedroom, to which we had instantly run, heard a voice that was much like my own.

"Signore, can I talk to your girl?"

"I *have* no girl," Signor Corelli said, "I only have sons."

"I saw her," she said. "Yesterday, at the window."

As soon as the girl had gone, Emilio burst upon us shouting, "You! You opened the blind! We told you *never* to open the blind." Signor Corelli entered the room. "Because of you," Emilio said, pointing to me, "we'll be shot."

My father held me close, my face against his chest. "Forgive us," he said. Then, releasing me from his grasp, turning me around so that we both were facing Signor Corelli, he said, "Signore, she's a child. I beg you. . . ."

Signor Corelli's face was suddenly red. "No, Professore, no, don't beg. Mine too is a child, big as he is. Don't beg." He sat beside us on the bed, groping for words and solutions. "But the girl has seen. She will surely tell her parents. Who knows what the parents will do. I hear there are bounties for turning in Jews. But she said she saw a girl— she didn't say there was a man. Professore," he said at last, "for you I know of no safer place, but let me take Rosanna to a convent."

Every week, Signor Corelli came to see me at the convent, and at each visit, the written message from my father was a group of pages taken from a score, sometimes one he'd composed himself, more often one by Puccini or Verdi. My answer was a set of lyrics of my own—labored over during all that week—and fitted to the music sent the prior week. For exactly five months. And when the Allies entered Rome and freed us, Signor Corelli came again, bringing my father to me.

We went to America, my father and I, to my uncle Beniamino who had left in '38, when the fascists passed the racial laws. My father never remarried. Signor Corelli's wife and younger sons returned to Rome, and his letters spoke about his wife, about their children's growing up and marriages and children, just as my father's letters spoke of me and mine. And there were photographs, of course.

Then my father died. I wrote and told Signor Corelli, and he answered at once, a letter filled with regret. Later, the Signora Corelli died too, and I, in turn, answered, and then continued to write. I had anglicized my name, and now that my father was gone, only Signor Corelli called me by the name "Rosanna."

Then it was Emilio who sent me a note. Papà is alive, Signora, but not well, and asked me to tell you that soon he will write. He has broken his thighbone—but soon, the doctors assure him, soon he'll be back on his feet.

He was eighty-four. He was of peasant stock, he had five years of schooling, and as a boy he was told we had killed his Lord. He became the tramway worker Angelo Corelli, and he was my last, indeed my truest link with my father, my past and the Italy that for hundreds of years had accepted its Jews.

The passport office helped, cooperated quickly, and I went to Rome.

On the phone, Emilio, disbelieving, asked, "In Rome?" And then, "Signora, how kind you are, how grateful I am. But that you traveled so far—he'll think it means that soon he'll die."

"But Signore," I said, "I've thought of that myself. I'm no longer the child who opened the blind." And at once I was sorry. It was something my father would never have said.

But he did not reproach me for the reference to the past

or ask me how I'd shield his father against the surprise. He left his office at once, and as he reached the lobby and approached, his hand outstretched and his smile as welcoming as any smile I had ever seen, I felt a rush of joy I hadn't expected to feel.

He had a compliment for me, and I for him, this handsome and cared-for Italian male in his carefully tailored Italian clothes. And as he drove us to the hospital we talked of families—he and my husband are both engineers—and of Italian politics, which my father had followed minutely as long as he lived.

Then, suddenly, he was solemn. "Signora, may I use the familiar form of address?" When I said "Of course," he said, "Rosanna, I'm sorry. I think about those days from time to time, especially now that Papà is sick. It was a time to be brave. Some people were, and some were not. I was not. Forgive me."

"Emilio, you were a child!" I said, but he wouldn't let me excuse him, wouldn't let me finish the sentence—"No," he said, shaking his head, "I was eighteen."

He preceded me into the hospital room, promising only to tell his father someone had come from afar, someone he didn't expect. And when I entered, Signor Corelli knew me at once.

"*Carissimo* Signore," I said, "I was on my way to Israel, and I couldn't bear to be so close to you and not stop off."

It was hard. He was tired. And letters are often easier. In minutes he was sleeping, and Emilio and I sat there quietly, Emilio whispering once, "He drops off, but a minute later he's awake."

I was assessing the room's equipment when I heard Signor Corelli muttering barely audible sounds. His eyes were shut. A moment later they were open wide and ablaze with amusement and mischief. "Rosanna!" he said. "What did we eat?"

"Eat?" I asked.

"Eat! What did we eat for dinner just before I took you to the convent?"

I turned for a moment to Emilio, who looked as surprised by the question as I. "I don't remember, Signore," I said.

"Emilio!" he said, pursuing the quiz, "What did we eat?"

Emilio laughed aloud and, with a catch in his voice, said, "You're asking *me?*"

"Peas!" his father said—triumphant over us both. Then he was quiet a moment or two, resting, the laughter gone from his eyes, but his face content. "And there weren't enough," he continued. "Remember what we would do during the war? We didn't eat only the peas—we ate the pods, even the pods."

"I had forgotten, Signore," I said, "but now I remember."

And it was true—I did, vividly. I had stripped the inner shell out of the pods, so that we could cook the tender outer part. And now, for the first time in years, I remembered some other details: that after we'd finished our food, I gathered the plates and forks, and for the last time in that modest room I scrubbed and dried them, slowly, delaying, while my father, Signor Corelli and Emilio watched me, each with his own conflicting thoughts that I as a child couldn't imagine, and all of them silent, smoking cigarettes.

Florence, May '86

I went to Settignano first, to Santa Marta's—the school that late in '43, when I was ten, was a convent school for boys. I talked with Sister Amedea, but we didn't remember each other at all, nor did I remember the bombing that shattered her arm. I did, however, remember the high stone wall between the school itself and the road that winds beside it down the hill, and the little stone lions along the path that's just inside that wall, and more. But what I recognized profoundly—as if I were still that child—was the view of Florence, away in the distance, where my parents were hidden, I didn't know where. We had said good-bye in the center of the city, in the archbishop's palace, where we were assured that I would be safest hidden up at Santa Marta's, high in the Fiesolan hills.

And yesterday I stood before the convent of the Carmine, where the Germans found my mother in less than a week, while I, for nine months afterward, looked backward toward the city, thinking she still was there. My father—on the morning after the raid in which she was caught—emerged from hiding, from a building on the Via del Leone close to the Carmine, and walked across the city and away into the hills, and sat on the ground near Santa Marta's, huddled against the cold stone wall. And later, having spoken to no one, walked back to his room.

I saved the bridge—the Ponte Vecchio—almost for last, each time stopping short of reaching it, walking from our own consulate beside the Arno to the British one, farther along on the Arno, and at each of them I stood at a bit of a distance, watching the Carabinieri on guard. I've been wanting to take their pictures, but, merely by wagging a finger at me, they induced me to stop. In the evening they leave, replaced by men of the Celere—equally armed. These two consulates, together with the Florence synagogue, appear to be the only places under threat of bombing in this peaceful city where most of the time I've been fully at ease.

And finally the Ponte Vecchio. I didn't want to look in the windows of stores. What I wanted to see was the bust of Cellini—or rather the space that surrounds it. It was there that from time to time my father would come on a Saturday morning. There at the statue, Don Leto Casini, a priest as innocent-looking as any tourist, would be waiting with money provided by Jews, to be given to other Jews, for food or whatever their need—at the risk of his life.

Nearby, if it has been rebuilt—a sudden rainstorm sent me running, leaving this part of my journey undone—would be the Church of Santo Stefano al Ponte. It doesn't appear on my map, but it does appear, however briefly, in the

memoirs, recently published, of the now Monsignor Casini. It was by the very old and dignified priest of Santo
Stefano that Don Casini—before the first of his two arrests
by the Germans, and therefore before he was using the
bridge—had been granted the use of a room. In this room,
on Saturday mornings, Jews assembled for Hebrew pray-
ers.

Later, as the Germans retreated, they let Ponte Vecchio
stand but bombed the buildings adjacent, so that the rubble, falling onto the bridge, would block the Allied advance.
The aged priest of Santo Stefano, warned beforehand to
leave, had refused, and when the Germans were gone and
the rubble cleared, he was found, sitting upright in his
armchair in the study, still supremely dignified, and dead.

Monsignor Casini, however, confesses now to "cowardice." He hadn't informed the priest he'd be giving the room
to Jews. He wanted it, he'd said, for unfortunate people in
need of a place to pray and be helped.

"Pay attention," the old man said. "Might there be among
them Jews?"

"Only poor unfortunates," he answered, and now in his
memoirs writes, "thereby calming my conscience and him."

When I had read that page, I asked my father, "Why do
you think Don Casini didn't admit you were Jews?"

"It's there in black and white," my father said. "He says
'for various reasons,' not the least of which was that he
didn't want to burden this old, venerable man."

"But why does he call it 'cowardice'?"

"You're reading the book," he said with a trace of pique,
"you can see for yourself. He deprecates himself. Don Casini *always* deprecates himself. But with a twinkle in his eye,
like when he tells about his childhood pranks. It was a

little nothing in his eyes, a little trick."

"For his childhood tricks he uses the words *marachelle, birichinate,* and what you call the 'twinkle' is very clear. For this he uses *vigliaccheria.* Cowardly act."

I stopped. I wanted to say, Was he afraid that if this particular priest had known the help was for Jews he might have refused? Like when the Archbishop of Perugia had shown him the door? But though the question troubled me, indeed weighed very heavily on me, I didn't. If my father, for my sake, has always suppressed a show of anxiety, then I, for his, must do the same.

"*Ask* him," he said. "You're going soon to Florence—if you have to ask him, you can ask him."

And now I can. The traffic along the Lungarno covers the sound as I ring the bell, and the door before me opens at once, as if he's been standing there waiting for me. I say simply, "Monsignore," and he answers, "How tall!"

He offers me food, something to drink, asks about my father's health, waves away any talk of our debt—"Too much honored," he tells me, "too much honored already."

I protest. I take from my pocket recent pictures of the tree that long ago was planted in his honor in Jerusalem, on the Avenue of the Righteous, and he looks at them with pleasure he doesn't attempt to disguise. He lifts his eyes toward mine, and softly he says, "*È cresciuto*"—It has grown. From a drawer nearby he takes a pair of earlier pictures of the tree—one from the time of planting and another one from ten years later—and repeats, "*È cresciuto.*"

He wants to talk about the present, not the past, but as

he utters the word *passato*, that question of mine returns to my mind. But now it's he who is old, and I know my question might ask him to say what he'd rather not have to reveal. And what I start to feel—only now—is that I just don't care enough any more, that any knowledge I might gain from asking it, though it would satisfy my curiosity, isn't worth the price he might pay.

Instead, I say, "Monsignore, please, a moment more on the past. In your memoirs, there isn't a word about fear. Were you afraid?"

"When I was arrested," he says with a smile, "if they had told me, 'tomorrow you'll be shot,' I'd have been a happy man, because what I dreaded, what I kept envisioning, was that they would hang me with barbed wire."

The image chills me, and for several seconds we both are silent. Then his smile widens, and with a dancing light in his eyes that my father would label a "twinkle," he says, "And if so? A minimal loss."

I'm sure my failure to laugh expresses dissent sufficiently well. I merely keep my eyes on his, and I know what I'll tell my father tonight on the phone. He won't admit he too would like to know about the priest of Santo Stefano. He'll only ask, "Is Don Casini well?" And I'll answer, "Yes, he's just fine, Dad, and he sends you his best." And then I'll add, "You were right about him all along, you know. He's exactly as you remember he was."

And I know that he'll ask me nothing more.

By Evil
and Kindness

I had gone to a party that Sylvie was giving for Reuben, where Sylvie, using the phrase as if she had coined it, wanted Reuben to "see and be seen." She admitted she really knew little about him, but she had loved him years before when he, her therapist then, had been "straightening out" her head. Now he was widowed, had relinquished his practice and escaped the northern winters, and before he was "caught" by someone unworthy, Sylvie had chosen some suitable women—one widowed, one divorced and one still married but deserted—and set them out before him against a background of married pairs.

I was meant to be half of a pair, but, only an hour before, my husband and I had quarreled, which Sylvie instantly guessed on seeing me enter alone. "My poor Rosanne," she said, asking me nothing at all to help her determine whose fault the quarrel had been. That is Sylvie's way: she

knows almost nothing of why I am as I am, but knowing
the single fact that I lost my mother in the camps, she
assumes I've again been wronged, carelessly dealt with by
everyone else, all my wounds—however she might picture
them—opened anew. I never reveal any more to her than
to anyone else, but in my gratitude for her compassion, I
overlook in her what in others puts me off.

Reuben, informed in advance of Sylvie's plan, thought I
was one of the three he should "see," and after we'd been
introduced to each other by somebody other than Sylvie,
he stayed with me, because, as he shamelessly told me later,
"the younger the better."

Sylvie, whose plan was impeded by Reuben's attention
to *me*, hurried to our side, smilingly called me a saboteur—
so that Reuben saw his mistake—and then, in turning
quickly away to conceal her annoyance, struck her hand
on a cabinet door.

Looking from her injured hand to me, she said "Damn!"
I, astonished at being the object of Sylvie's anger, said
nothing at all, even when I heard her say—petulantly,
mournfully—"My *nail* is shot," and even a moment later
when she added, "Now it has to be wrapped."

With apparently genuine interest, Reuben asked her,
"Wrapped?"

Softening a little, Sylvie said, "My fingernail broke.
Haven't you heard of wrapping a nail?"

A look came into Reuben's eyes that Sylvie, I knew at
once, did not understand—of disbelief, followed quickly
not by laughter but by bitterness, perhaps indeed by anger.
It said exactly what I heard inside myself when Sylvie started
mourning her nail. Even when she took him by the elbow
toward her chosen three and I was left to others—cheerful

as I almost always seem, but as almost always concealing
an impulse toward rage—I couldn't forget that uncensored
look.

My interest in Reuben grew, and I watched him, attracted
despite his age, because I was sure—although, as happens
with so much else that we know, it was something other
than reason that made me so sure—that there was a bond
between us of similar loss. At last, when I saw him break
away from one of Sylvie's three, I put myself into his path.

He was polite, but he seemed distracted now, and I lost
my resolve. Then, in a thoroughly unprecedented move—
seized by my isolation, and yearning for closeness with
someone of my own kind—I rejected every inhibition, asking, "Reuben, where were you in '44?"

If he was surprised by the question, his surprise didn't
show. "Nowhere," he said, "where you might have been."

I was hurt, but, having gone this far, I couldn't stop.

"Probably not," I said. "I was in a convent in Rome."

He didn't answer at once, but when at last he did he only
said, "How old were you?"

"Twelve."

He took my arm and led me out of the room to the end
of the hall, where others could see us, but where they would
have to think and decide before they'd intrude.

"I was twenty-six," he said. "In Castiglione, outside
Florence. Living openly with false papers and a long Italian
name. With a priest named Don Giulio. How did you get
to the convent?"

"How did you find Don Giulio?"

"It was he who did the finding. I was a Polish national
but had studied medicine in Genoa and knew Italian. In
'43, I was living in Trieste, but I fled when the Germans

arrived. I headed south, toward Rome in fact, but stopped in Florence and went for advice to Nathan Cassuto, the rabbi. He sent me to the archbishop's palace, and from there I was sent to a priest, who kept me with two other Jews in a room in his church."

"And Don Giulio?"

"His parish was out in the country, where there was food. Once a week he would pack up a suitcase—a bread, a chicken, vegetables from his mother's garden—and go on the bus to the city, where food, as you of course know, was terribly scarce. He would divide up the food among friends, priests like himself. On one of his trips, he found us with one of these friends and offered to take one of us back. And you? How did you get to the convent?"

"We were hidden, my father and I, until I was seen at a window. The man who was hiding us took me to where he believed I'd be safe. I was lucky."

"*How* lucky?" he asked.

"Only my mother and sister," I said. "During the raid in Rome."

"I'm sorry, Rosanne," he said. "*My* mother and sister were saved. They were hidden in the Convent of La Calza, in Florence, but left for a couple of hours to go to the synagogue. While they were there the Germans arrived. My mother and sister saw them and ran. They knew where I was and managed to get to Don Giulio's too."

Ridiculous pictures entered my mind, of *my* mother and sister, still in their nightclothes, holding hands and fleeing in the chilly dawn from Rome, northward and into the Tuscan countryside, meeting with Reuben's mother and sister and reaching Don Giulio's too.

"And they lived there as you did?" I asked. "Openly?"

"Only I could live that way," he said. "He had told everyone, even his parents—they lived with him, and his mother kept house—he said I was a friend from seminary days, but one who hadn't become a priest. He said I'd been sick and needed a place to recover, and no one doubted the story at all. His parents discovered the truth when my mother and sister arrived, because my mother didn't speak Italian. She and my sister had to be hidden.

"And you know, Rosanne?" he said with a smile, "there was another priest there, living in the house, a man whose courage Don Giulio didn't believe he could trust. He never discovered my mother and sister were there. During the day a servant would take them their food, and at night Don Giulio'd let them come out of their room and into a garden back of a wall."

The smile faded from his face, and I wanted to ask him whom he had lost, but as I breathed the initial sound of "whom," he started speaking again.

"One evening, Rosanne, I went to my mother's and sister's room. Out on the table there was this strange-looking bread. I stared—it was like no other bread I'd ever seen—and my mother said, 'Don Giulio's mother baked it for us. Did you know that such kindness still could exist?'

" 'I know it only because of them,' I said. I picked up the knife, but when I tried to cut with it, it slid from the crust. 'What's wrong with this bread?' I asked. 'Why won't it cut?'

"My mother said, 'Don't you know what day this is? It's beginning of Passover, Reuben—Don Giulio told her.'

"Don Giulio's mother—this simple old woman—she was a peasant who, until she met *me,* had never known a Jew, and she baked us this bread." I didn't answer, and Reuben, thinking I hadn't understood, explained, "An unleavened bread."

We stood together, Reuben and I, silent, but linked—in this houseful of sheltered American Jews—by the evil and kindness we both had known. As if we were one, we turned—suddenly aware of Sylvie. She was down at the end of the hall, far out of range of our voices, but watching, as excluded from our community as we have felt from hers, and vulnerable—as hesitant as an unwanted intuitive child. I too was hesitant, but I lifted my arm and held it out to include her as well as I could.

Not yet able to smile, I said, "We were coming, Sylvie. I didn't mean to keep him all day to myself."

It was she who relaxed and smiled. She waited until we had reached her and said. "Aren't *you* the surprise, Rosanne." She turned to Reuben. "Normally she doesn't put much stock in therapists. What did you get so chummy about?"

"Bread," he said. "Matzo, in fact."

"Oh you're crazy, Reuben," she said, "I don't believe that you and Rosanne got glued together on food."

"Really," he said, "it was a matzo. Among other things."

But she didn't ask about the other things. She was our hostess of course and therefore busy—attentive to what she believed were our needs. She was bent on giving us food and wine in lovely surroundings, with peaceful music softly played, and pleasant conversation, and alliances against aloneness—doing her best to enrich our lives. Nor has she asked about those other things since. Nor have Reuben or I, in fact, been able to ask her why not.

Vincenzo
and Giulia

Vincent stopped, stunned by the sight of the child. A three-year-old, dark, with an oval face, cleft chin and remarkable eyes—almond-shaped, large and strikingly green. She stood at a rack of souvenir tee shirts, rigid, her arms at her sides, her head turned up, and turning only her eyes she called, "Mama? Mama?"

Around him on Olvera Street the tourists were strolling and eyeing the stalls, inspecting sombreros, knitted capes, clay pots, but parting for Julia and him like a slow-moving stream would part at a rock. The child turned, revealing a side of her face. Near her ear was a small brown mole.

"Mama?" she called, and then more frightened, louder, *"Donde, Mama, donde?"*

Vincent lunged, and the little girl shrieked. He fell to his knees and pulled her close, begging, *"Piccina, piccina, no no, non piangere,"* but the child, struggling, shrieked again.

He drew away, his hands leaving her just as her mother arrived.

"Bastard!" the Mexican woman screamed, "Why you touch?"

Seizing the woman's arm, Julia pleaded, "No, he called her 'little one,' he asked her not to cry, that's all he did."

"Why he hold her? I call the police!"

Raymond, Julia's and Vincent's son, was now at their side. He pulled his father erect and, pointing a finger inches away from the young, belligerent woman's nose, he threatened her softly, "I don't know what you want, but you'd better stop."

Now Chris, Raymond's son, stood beside them too, and Julia, strengthened by the presence of her son and grown-up grandson, dropped her pleading tone, advising the suddenly hesitant woman, "You should hold her hand."

In the quarter hour that followed, Vincent entered a separate world. He let himself be hurried into a taxi, and there unaware, it appeared, of his family's stares, he sat among them silent, his eyes directed down to the floor of the cab. Nor did he look around when they reached the hotel that Chris had been planning to show him. He merely let himself be led, till he was seated in the rooftop restaurant, where now a drink that Raymond had ordered was standing before him untouched.

"Look, Vincent," Julia said, "the Japanese garden. There's a pond on the roof. Look how the light from it comes through the windows and ripples up there on the ceiling."

Vincent seemed not even to hear, and Chris took over. "Pop? The restaurant's name? The Thousand Cranes? . . ."

Without looking up, but with a gesture of his hand, Vincent signaled that he stop. Chris could see his father and Julia exchange a glance of relief. He saw another signal, this one from Julia—to try for another response—but this he refused. He had seen Vincent's dignity destroyed, and fully aware of it only now, he was gripped by pity and love. His northern Italian "Pop," gray-haired but youthfully slender, and always distinguished-looking and strong, was the darling of them all.

"Sixty-five," Julia had said this morning, "is still a young age for a man. And Chris," she had added, "keep those college girls away. *This* man is mine."

But here Julia was tense, and with a decisive lift of her head, she banged her fist on the table, hard. Vincent looked up. Two of the Japanese waitresses turned, looked, and then, as if nothing untoward had occurred, turned away.

"No more," Julia said. "You're going to tell me what happened back there."

Through clenched teeth, in a low voice, Raymond demanded, "Mom! What are you doing? Not here."

"I don't *care* what the waitresses think. Here! You and Chris are *here,* and you he doesn't ignore." She turned to Vincent. "Because of that child you were speaking Italian. For the first time in over thirty years. It has something to do with your secret—I want you to tell me, now!"

Vincent glanced at Raymond and Chris. Then, pointing his finger at Julia as Raymond had done to the Mexican woman, and in a voice that Julia remembered well but Raymond and Chris never had heard—cold, cruel, deadly—he answered, "Don't ever speak to me like that again."

He rose from the table and marched from the room, followed by Chris, leaving Julia, despite herself, embarrassed before the waitresses, while Raymond, unprepared, fumbled with his wallet for a suitably large tip.

In the lobby of their hotel downtown, at the elevators, Vincent left them without a word. Julia, for a moment hesitant, approached the Christmas tree. Raymond asked his son to follow Vincent, while he himself watched as Julia, elegant in her fine black suit, gently touched the tree's decorations—voluptuous satin bows, pink, that matched the pink poinsettias massed throughout the room. Soon she turned, scanned the quiet lobby and walked to a rose-colored sofa.

Raymond approached and sat down. "Mom? Don't let this come between you—this morning you were proud of him. And despite how he sounded, *he's* proud of *you.*" She smiled. "Why do you look like that?" he said. "Don't you believe me?"

"No."

"You turned yourself from a peasant to *this,*" he said, extending his hand. "Why would he *not* be proud?" She looked away. "I never saw you like this," he said. "Please! Don't sit here alone."

"Where should I go?"

"Go upstairs and talk to him."

"No."

"Then do it for Chris! He's waited for months for this visit—not just to show you his dorm, but to show you the rest of Los Angeles, introduce his roommate—everything's planned."

"For once in my life," she said, "I've rebelled against my husband, and my son is on *his* side."

"Rebelled? What have *you* had to rebel about?"

"When you were a boy—sick—and we took you to Fatima, I held you and walked on my knees for an hour, praying for you."

"So? It was *your* decision to make yourself suffer."

"I thought that something had happened that day, *aside* from your getting well. Between you and me, something lasting, that—no matter what we'd ever disagree on—there'd be something to count on. That we were brought together in a special way."

"We *are* together in a special way, and so are you and he, but he still has a right to some privacy even from you."

"Oh," she said, "there's that 'privacy' again. Well he's not entitled to it any more. I promised I'd never speak of my past and never question his, and I didn't, even when he did the *craziest* things. But not any more. If I still have to pay, I want to know why."

"Stop it, Mom, you're not paying. You started this whole thing. He was humiliated. Those people thought he'd *fondled* that child, and you, in front of Chris and me, ordering him around, you made it worse."

"I know. What *you* don't know is that I've paid for forty years. Because of him I left—deserted everyone I cared about at home. He took me back to Europe once, for that single day in Fatima, for the miracle, because I said if he didn't and then you died I'd kill myself. But then, so close to Italy, he wouldn't let me go home for even a day. Why? What happened to him there? Do you know that after we got here he wouldn't allow me to speak in Italian—to anyone? That till we both were speaking English well, we hardly spoke to each *other*? As if by blotting the past and even the language out of our lives we had done something good.

Why was it good? While some of the people I care for still are alive, why can't I go home?"

"Who could you have there today that's still so important to you? Nobody!"

"Nobody!"—repeating not only the word but his arrogant tone. "American sons, what do you know about family? And you in particular, Raymond, what do you know about *me?*" She did not understand these times or this country, where parents and children were so divided. Raymond was almost forty, and she had raised his son for him, and most of the time she could feel his impatience, or worse. She waved her hand—quickly, irritably. "Besides," she said, "I didn't want you to have any reason to hate him—I wanted him always to have your respect."

"Did *you* hate him?"

"Of course not!"

"Christ! For *you* to have secrets from *me* was okay, right? And *I'm* the guilty one because I couldn't read your mind." Julia flinched, and he felt a twinge of regret. Warily, he asked, "What did he do that was crazy?"

"I took an oath I wouldn't tell. But I have to know what's behind it all, and I can't put it off any more. I make very few demands on you, you know that, but I'm making one now. I want you to ask."

Raymond stood up and walked to the tree. He examined the satin bows, and when he came back he said, "I don't know what the little girl has to do with his speaking Italian again or with anything else, but I know my father does not molest children, and I don't have to know the rest. But if you feel you need to go back, *I* will take you. For now what he needs is a breather from us. You and I will go into the bar. We'll have a leisurely glass of wine, and then we'll go up to your room and tell him as soon as I can I'm taking you back."

Before she'd had time to refuse, Chris had arrived and was standing in front of them too. "Look, Dad," he said, "I know you asked me to stay with him, but it's not what he wants. He needs to be left by himself for a while."

"That's what I just told Momma," Raymond said, and extended his hand to help his mother stand up. She hesitated—long enough for them both to notice—but then accepted the help.

Sitting across a table from them, and becoming angrier still than she'd been only minutes before, Julia sipped her wine. Why, she wondered, had she come to the bar? She hadn't wanted to talk any longer to Raymond, and surely not about things that would lead to worrying Chris.

And then she knew exactly why: she hadn't wanted her grandson to know she'd reproached his father. Just as she'd always protected their image of Vincent, she now was protecting Raymond's as well. Why? She was indeed no longer a peasant, and she had learned, though not through any help of theirs, of her right to speak for herself. So why was she silent now? If Raymond, as he had said, had never seen her as she was today, why wasn't he aware of *her* pain as Chris had been aware of Vincent's?

All at once she perceived the fault as her own. She had waited for Vincent to *take* her home, implying she couldn't go back by herself. It was as if her life were split in two, as if when confronting events from the past she was bound by unbreakable habits of thought.

Holding herself responsible now, she felt some remorse, toward both Vincent and her son, but just as she felt it, Chris directed a worried, questioning glance at Raymond, and Raymond, with half-closed exasperated eyes, shrugged. The glance had asked, What's wrong? And the shrug had answered, Who cares?

"Chris," she said, "would you please take your father and leave me alone? I too have a lot to deal with today."

Raymond, insulted by being dismissed in the care of his son, stood up and said, "You have even more to deal with than you know." He turned and left, while Chris, for a moment indecisive, remained at the table with Julia.

Offended by her son, and touched by the worry in Chris's face—and by his not having followed his father—Julia brushed at the rims of her eyes.

"Momma, what's wrong?" Chris asked.

"Chris," she said, "when Pop asked you to leave, you left."

"Because I knew what was hurting him."

"Chrissie, please."

"Okay, Momma, but where will you be? Where should I look for you—will you be here?"

A chill came over her, lifting the hair on her arms. Similar words, but ringing with fear, were echoing back from the past in the voice of a child in a schoolroom in Rome.

"Momma?" he asked.

"I'll be right here, Chris, waiting for you."

He came to her side, put his arm about her shoulder and touched the side of his face to hers. Then he left.

She looked toward the door. Raymond was standing there, watching, fists on his hips. If I could live my life again, she thought, I wouldn't marry Vincent, and I wouldn't have that son. I'd marry a Roman workingman, or a peasant as simple as I was then, and I'd raise Italian children, who don't believe their mother's an enemy, or at best a fool. And I would be to Franco and Aldo as if they were mine.

It was four o'clock, Saturday morning, October 16, 1943. Giulia awoke to some unrecognizable sounds. Uneasy— waking in a place with which she wasn't fully familiar— she dressed and got ready to work. There was soon a series of taps on her door.

Before her was one of the building's tenants, a woman of eighty or more, dishevelled, disoriented, wearing the clothes in which she had slept.

"Signorina, the noises," she said. "Did you hear the noises?"

"I heard *something*," Giulia answered, "but I'm not sure what."

"Not far from here. Like marching."

"Then you thought so too."

"Could it be the Germans?"

"Why would they march while it's dark? Don't worry, it's nothing, I'm sure."

Giulia guided the woman back to the stairs, led her up and settled her into her bed.

"I've forgotten," the old woman said. "Your sister and her husband—how long will they stay in the village?"

"They didn't know, but just till my mother gets better, then they'll be back."

"But you—to be the janitor, to wash the stairs—how old can you be? Eighteen?"

"But it'll be good for my mother."

Without a pause, the woman asked, "Would you like a book?"

"A book?"

"Those," she said, "they're all in Hebrew—they were my husband's—but mine, over here, they're all in Italian. Novels, you see, I only read novels—I never read serious things. Would you like to have one of my books?"

"But . . . how kind. Which one?"

"Whichever you like. Pick, pick," the woman urged, "it'll be yours," and as Giulia opened one and then another book, the woman settled into her pillow and closed her eyes.

But not for long. It was half past five and turning light. Trucks came thundering into the street, and Giulia, followed by the old woman, went to the window to look. From their tires to their canvas roofs the trucks were black, and from one of them, now in front of the building, uniformed men jumped to the ground and started to pound on the large front door.

Giulia ran from the room and down to the door. The men had rifles with fixed bayonets, and one of them carried a list from which he informed the others of which of the building's apartments to search. Ignored and stupefied, Giulia stood in the hallway and watched. One of the Germans knocked on a door nearby—loudly, steadily—until it opened and a man, partially dressed and barely awake, stood before him and stared. The German thrust a notice before him and briskly marched to another door. Giulia went back to her own apartment, took her identity card and returned to the elderly woman.

"Signora," she said, "don't be afraid—I'll stay with you. I don't know what it is, but it has something to do with Jews."

And what it had to do with Jews became engraved on Giulia's mind. A typewritten list of instructions, in both

German and Italian, and intended for the Jewish tenant,
was placed instead into Giulia's hand. She read it aloud:

Together with your family and with the other Jews belong-
ing to your house, you will be transferred. You must take
along food for at least eight days, ration cards, identity cards
and drinking cups. You may take a small valise with personal effects, blankets, money and jewels. Lock the apartment and take the key with you. The sick, even the gravest
cases, may not, for any reason, remain behind. There are
infirmaries in the camp. Twenty minutes after receiving this
notice the family must be ready to leave.

"What?" the old woman asked.

Giulia rummaged around the apartment, filled a valise
and said, "Now listen! You must do the rest by yourself.
Gather your money and papers, and don't forget your key—
remember your key. I'm going upstairs to the young signora. A week ago—you remember? A baby was born."

But instead of chaos surrounding the newborn, there was
a studied, deliberate calm. The husband and wife already
were dressed. The woman, hardly older than Giulia, was
nursing the infant. The man was packing the bags.

Giulia returned to the lower floor, where people were
running, weeping, some of them still only partially dressed.
A German stood at the head of the stairs, calling, *"Raus!
Raus!"*

The old woman, bent by the weight of her bag, arrived
at his side. Turning her head, she noticed that Giulia was
there and stopped. "Your book," she said. "We forgot about
your book," and started searching her pockets, muttering,
"Where is my key? Did I lock the door?"

She left her valise and started to turn, but the German, mindful that twenty minutes had passed, took her shoulders, as if assessing her weight, and with a practised shove delivered her in three resounding thumps right to the foot of the stairs.

He waited for several seconds and sent her valise.

Giulia's hands were gripping the sides of her head, and as the German turned, she said, *"Non sono ebrea"*—I'm not a Jew. She forgot she had brought her identity card, and before he could answer, ducked around him and hurried down.

Out in the street, two of the Germans were pushing the crumpled old woman onto the truck. Giulia remembered and now produced her identity card. *"Sono cattolica—non sono ebrea."* The men, it appeared, did not understand and, ignoring her papers, pointed up to the truck.

She turned to ask if someone could translate, and in doing so, jostled the people behind her—the couple with the child. They were standing erect and serene, and their strength, which she sensed was achieved through an act of will, made her ashamed. Quickly she turned and mounted the truck.

Slumped forward, held in place by the people beside her, was the old woman, her face hidden from view. Visible, however, was the young mother, who resumed nursing her child. Out of the depths of what she later called her peasant intuition, Giulia knew that none of them—neither the old woman nor the young couple and their infant child—would need their keys again.

The truck soon stopped at another building, and another group of families were pushed aboard. One of the women held in her arms a baby of less than a year. A boy whom Giulia judged to be at least two, together with an older girl, were huddled against the woman and holding on to her dress.

"Signora," Giulia murmured, "I'm not a Jew. I'm sure I'll go free. Let me take your little ones." The woman flinched and averted her eyes. "Not the girl," Giulia said. "She's too old—she couldn't be mine."

The woman remained as she'd been, silent, but after a while she lowered her head and started to cry. Minutes before the truck had stopped at its goal, a school near the Tiber, she handed the baby to Giulia, saying simply, "Aldo." Giulia settled the baby in one of her arms and extended her other hand. To Giulia's waiting hand the woman delivered the hand of the boy, saying, "Franco."

As they entered the Collegio Militare, the Jewish woman had a daughter, and Giulia had two small sons. But that night, the five of them rested together on straw in a room of the school. The mother instructed the boy to be good, to leave her and go—and without looking back—when Giulia said it was time. The boy, frightened, asked, "But where will you be? How will you know where to find me?"

Julia finished her wine. Oh, Franco, where are you and Aldo now? And Vincent—is he as inaccessible to me as the two of you? Would I really not marry him today if I were young? And at this time of my life, would I have the courage to leave him?

Alone upstairs in their room, Vincent sat at the desk and wrote in Italian.

Carissimo Don Viale,

Forgive me. Though I haven't written you in years, I think of you often. It's you I've admired, indeed revered, above everyone except my brother.

Nor have I forgotten the woman and child. There are times when I can forget them, sometimes even for weeks, but then they return, for no discernible reason, and leave me again, as quietly as they came. But there have been times they seem to *insist* there's a reason—as they did today.

He found it hard to go on, and stopped.

It was the night between the eighth and the ninth of September 1943. He was retreating through the Alps from France, going along a wide road. All around him there were Jews, leaving what had been the safety of St. Martin Vesubie—occupied till then by Italy—and fleeing, as now his army itself was fleeing, before the German advance.

He heard a child complaining in French, "I'm so tired— *why* must we follow the soldiers?"

The answer came in a woman's resolute voice. "Because the soldiers are Italian, and are going home, and we must stay with them, because they're good."

He stopped abruptly and turned, blocking their way. The woman was older than he—in her middle or even late twenties—and had a distinctively beautiful, angular face. She didn't appear to resent his gaze—she smiled—but he, embarrassed by showing himself attracted to her, turned to look down at the child. She was peering up at him with large unforgettable eyes—almond-shaped and brilliantly green.

In perfect French, but with an Italian accent, he asked the child, "Would you like me to carry you, so you can sleep?"

"Ah, non, monsieur," her mother said, "she's just a little tired—there's really no need—but you are so kind to offer, and, truly, we thank you."

"But this part of the march is . . ."—he searched for the word in French—"deceptive! Do you know the elevation at the pass? She'll be exhausted—hours before you get through, let alone before you get down to Valdieri."

She put her suitcase down by the side of the road. "Yes. But you, do go on. Your kindness has shown what I've told her already: after we cross into Italy, then we can rest."

Convinced that she thought him only a boy, he nodded and left, without even glancing again at the child.

He climbed the narrowing road slowly, passing comrades, some in uniform and others like himself already rid of it, and passing refugees like her, well-dressed, speaking in German or French. But there were other Jewish refugees among them from the east—Poland and elsewhere—shabbily dressed, and speaking a language he never had heard till recently, but similar enough to German so that, some of it at least, he understood.

The road became increasingly steep, and now beside him was a family with six or seven children, the father and sons with odd-looking curls swinging along near their ears. In the cold and dark of the mountain trail, one of the boys, the smallest, struggled forward and wept. His mother was holding an infant. His father, brothers and sisters were carrying bags.

Vincenzo stopped and picked up the boy, who at once was asleep, and to the mother's grateful words he merely nodded. He trudged along, but the path was even more tortuous now, and narrower, and the only light the occasional flash of a match. To both left and right there were terrible drops.

Abruptly, he set the boy on the ground and, avoiding the bewildered, sleep-befuddled face, turned back. When he met the woman at last, the valise she had held was gone, and she was carrying her daughter. He held out his arms, and she handed over the child, who opened her eyes for a moment and then, burying her forehead in his neck, went back to sleep.

"Thank you," the woman said.

"She seems hot," he answered.

"I didn't now she had a fever till I picked her up. Had you gone far?"

"No, but you have to stop and rest. The climb gets steep."

He lowered himself to the ground slowly, so as not to waken the child. The woman knelt, removed her coat and, as Vincenzo hungrily watched, her sweater as well. She wrapped the sweater around her daughter's coat, tucking it between Vincenzo's chest and the child's. At the touch of her hand, Vincenzo was filled with desire.

As she sat down, he asked, "Where's your husband?"

"In France—the German zone—looking for his sister."

"He was out of there, and he went *back?*

"He was trying to bring her to Italy's zone."

"That was insane!" he said.

"No. The Vichy police demanded you give us to *them,* but you, you Italians, your army refused."

"I know! So wasn't it crazy for him to go back?"

"Isn't that what *you've* done for *me?*—a stranger to you?"

"No! I'm not a Jew, and I didn't go back to the Germans."

"Yes, you're right," she said. "But we didn't know that Italy would sign an armistice. That its army would have to retreat before he got back."

He flushed. "Of course. You probably think I'm a fool."

"A fool? Oh, if only everyone. . . ." She shook her head. Then, as if to reassure him, she asked, "May we use the familiar form of address?"

He felt a dizzying surge of joy. "Yes!" he said, loudly, so that the little girl pulled her forehead away from his neck and looked with astonishment into his eyes. He put his hand to the side of her face where he felt—and inspected—a small, brown mole at the tip of her ear. And again she lowered her head and slept. Softly, he added, "My name is Vincenzo."

"And mine Claudine."

"Enchanté," he said.

Some moments of awkward silence passed.

"Of my husband's family," she said at last, "his sister is the only one whose whereabouts we know."

"Where in France are you from?"

"We're Belgian," she said.

"You've fled from there to France and now to Italy?"

"Yes. But others have come from farther away. Do *you* have a family?"

"Parents, and an older brother, a Socialist—always a step ahead of the Fascists."

"Now that your country's out of the war, what will you do?"

"Go home to my family. Mussolini's gone—Italy's free of him at last, and soon the Allies will win."

Hopefully, she asked, "Do you really think they'll win?"

"Of course. Why else are all of you following us?"

"Because for us, back there is certain death. Maybe it's waiting in Italy too, but, despite your racial laws, it doesn't seem likely—not from the way you Italians acted in France." She crossed her arms on her chest. "Vincenzo, I'm cold. Are you rested enough to go on?"

He stood up carefully, his hand on the child's head to keep her in place. "Claudine," he said, "the road ahead is narrow, and with gorges everywhere, so I have to talk to you now. I'll take you through the pass and settle you down in the valley. Then I'll go home to Milan, but as soon as I can I'll be back."

"Vincenzo, don't," she said. "My husband will survive—I'm sure. In St. Martin Vesubie, many older people stayed—they were sure if they left they'd die on the road. They'll tell him which of the passes I chose, and he'll know where to look."

Late in the evening of September tenth, they reached Valdieri and found a hotel were Vincenzo left Claudine and the child. He slept for a while and wandered around in the valley hearing the news and making his plans, and when he saw Claudine at last, she already had heard—as he too had heard—that the Germans hadn't stopped at the Alps. They had occupied the north of Italy, and she was now as much at risk in the Gesso Valley as her husband was at risk in France.

"Some of the others have left to hide in the mountains," she said, "but . . . ," pointing to the little girl, "I need a doctor, not a cave."

"I've been to Borgo San Dalmazzo," he said, "to the priest, a certain Don Viale. He'll find a family willing to hide you."

"A family? Why would they risk the lives of their children for *us?* Do you know what the Germans will do if they find us?"

"Do you really think I don't know?"

"I'm sorry," she said, "I didn't mean to insult you. But in France you had an army, you were Germany's ally then, you could defy them. Here we'd be with individuals—who don't have power—whom we don't even know. And forgive me, Vincenzo, but the Church has taught them . . . well, you know what I mean."

"These people are unknown to *us,* but not to this priest. The Fascists imprisoned him. Once, trying to kill him, they ran him down with a truck. Argue with *him* if you must."

But when she repeated her fears to Don Viale, he answered, "You and Vincenzo have lived a privileged life. You've had wealth, education, aspirations. The people to whom I send you have had nothing but their lives, and keeping alive is all they can hope for. You and your child are doing the same—only trying to live—and the people will help."

He left her there with Don Viale and went to Milan. It was mid-September. The Germans discovered the prison to which

Mussolini—so recently ousted—was sent, and they freed him. They gave him a new but republican Fascist state which ordered the army back into service. Some anti-Fascists who, prematurely, had been celebrating Mussolini's fall, were imprisoned, and among them was Vincenzo's brother.

In October he found him. A guard escorted Vincenzo in silence, unlocked a cell and left. His brother was in it alone, curled on the floor in bloody clothes, and what should have been his eyes resembled purple eggs.

Vincenzo drew away. Then, forcing himself to look at his brother's face, and kneeling close but afraid to touch, he said, "Rinaldo? Rinaldo, it's me."

"Oooooh, no," he heard. "The bastards—they let you in."

"Tell me," he said. "Tell me what to do."

"Go away. I can't bear that you see me this way."

"*I* couldn't bear to *leave* you this way."

"Please. It was bad enough before. But these *repubblichini* are the dregs of Italy. Go. Fight. *Please* don't get caught."

But he didn't go at once. He tried to remove his brother's shirt, which was stuck to one of his shoulders by blood, and the flesh came away from the bone.

He fled to the mountains, pursued by Rinaldo's image: eyes, huge and swollen shut, like purple eggs. Sticky blood. The shoulder's flesh. And by his plea: "Don't get caught." He joined a partisan band and hid in a cave, doing minor damage to the Germans here and there, always anxious, fearing reprisals against the local people, and waiting for the Allied troops to reach the north and allow him to join them. And then he learned about the order posted in the valley weeks before—on the eighteenth of September—by the German S.S. Command:

By eighteen hundred today, all foreigners in Borgo San Dalmazzo and its surrounding towns must present themselves to the German Command, mountain barracks.

After this time, all foreigners who have not presented themselves will be immediately shot.

The same penalty will fall on anyone in whose habitation said foreigners are found.

"She's strong, in a way," Don Viale said. "She was sure she'd be caught and everyone shot, so she gave herself up."

In a sudden rage against Claudine, he roared, *"Gave up?* She could have hidden in the mountains, like others did."

"Perhaps, but the child, though she was better, wasn't strong. And with winter approaching, the cold up there was a threat. In the camp their life is hard, but it's endurable, and for the little girl it seemed to the mother safer by far."

His anger subsiding, he said, "She has a husband. Has he come to you looking for her?"

"No, and I don't think he will, even if he does get back to southern France. The S.S. are not only searching the houses. They're snatching whoever they find in the streets. They examine the men, and the circumcised they ship to Drancy on the next train out. And from Drancy they go to the east."

"And in the camp," he asked, "is there a way to escape?"

"Many have," Don Viale said. "Many already have."

Hidden by Don Viale, Vincenzo stayed. Venturing out at night to the outskirts of town. From a distance inspecting the camp. The barracks. The autumn countryside. Questioning. Looking for how to arrange an escape.

On November twenty-first, just past noon, a message from Don Viale: They are all at the station, being deported today.

When Vincenzo arrived at the heart of the town, there were prisoners still coming in. In the cold. In the rain. In the black day's darkness. Slowly, on foot. In unearthly silence. Dragging valises and bundles. Some of them carrying children. Others the sick on stretchers. Beside them and armed, the S.S.

On the tracks, refrigerator cars. Airtight. Ten of them. Twelve. On the platform, chaos. Horrific noise. Children's cries. Frantic babble. German shouts. Onto the car! Fifty per car! Old and young. Pushed by rifles. Cars sealed up.

There! Close to the train, Claudine and the child.

The German loading the refugees turns, distracted—one of his comrades has called. He moves away from Claudine and the child. The child is suddenly rigid, arms at her sides. Her voice in his ears like a roar: "Where, Mama, where?"

Claudine bends down. Picks her up. Hushes her. Turns. Sees Vincenzo. Vincenzo! Holds her out to him. Holds her out to him. Images—rising in the space between Claudine and him: Rinaldo curled on the prison floor. Eyes like purple eggs. Sticky blood. Shoulder flesh. "Don't get caught." Holds her out to him. "Don't get caught." Holds her out to him. "Don't get caught." The child cries, "Mama? Mama?" The German returns.

It's too late.

Vincent resumed his letter to Don Viale.

> Do you remember what we said that night? I
> wept, because my brother's wounds, which
> should have made me strong, had made me a
> coward instead.
>
> I told you then that I couldn't see how a
> man of intelligence still could believe in a per-
> sonal God. That's how I feel even now, but
> there's something that tears at me from the
> other direction: the persistence of what I've tried
> to call "coincidence."
>
> I saw the child today. I know, of course,
> that it really was *not* that child, but even if my
> memory is blurred a bit by time, they were
> enough alike that I have to confront their alike-
> ness, asking, *Why* did this child appear in my
> path? Was this nothing but coincidence? She
> wasn't like Claudine's in features alone—she
> was also rigid with fear. And she said exactly
> what Claudine's had said, what I had heard—
> clearly—in spite of everything: "Where, Mama,
> where?"
>
> What does this mean? Were you right after
> all? Is there indeed a God? Is He speaking to me
> through this child? And the other, earlier coinci-
> dence—that *Giulia* was put in my path. Can it
> really have been—as I've tried to believe—for no
> reason at all? Only through chance?

Who can recall the details when forty years have elapsed?

Only the outlines remain: the Allies' delay as they battled their way from the south; the British bombers striking the north; the minor partisan efforts one hoped would have major effects; traveling by night and hiding by day on the journey to Rome and south of it, desperate because of wasted time, searching for a small unguarded place to cross the front and join the Allied troops. Minor details are forgotten.

Remembered: Giulia when he saw her first: barely eighteen and already a widow with two small sons. Her eyes were fearful at first, suspicious, and the skin of her forehead a little discolored, as if from a bruise.

"Come in, Signora," he said. Grasping the coat of the boy at her side, she shook her head. "Believe me," he said, "I'm Pietro's cousin. Ada said you might come. Don't be afraid."

Hesitant, she followed him in, saying, "I wasn't afraid."

"They didn't tell me you're young." She settled the baby down on the floor. "About your husband," he said, "I'm sorry. He was killed in Africa?"

She nodded. "About me—did Ada say anything else?"

"That you work in a building where Jews were arrested. That you're somehow related to her—I didn't quite follow—I had only just come, and I wanted to sleep."

"You're hiding? A deserter?"

"No," he answered. "Wounded."

"If you could, would you fight on the side of the Germans again?"

"If you were a man, would *you?*"

"No."

"Because they started a war and your husband was killed?"

"No."

"Then why not?"

"Because."

"Signora," in his tone a hint of apology now, "Yes, I'm in hiding. I tried to get through to the Allies, but couldn't."

"I know. Wounded or not, if you still would fight on the side of the Fascists, Pietro wouldn't have taken you in."

She returned to visit them often, always of course with the children and always when Ada was there. He would find she was watching him closely and turning away when he noticed, but it still was Claudine he desired.

A day came, however, when Giulia arrived distraught and broke into sobs. "At Palazzo Braschi, *repubblichini*— Italians! With whips!"

"The dregs of Italy," he said, and, hearing himself repeat what Rinaldo had said, he turned and bowed his head, overcome. And Giulia, seeing his anguish, handed the baby to Ada, went to him, and held him in her arms.

On the fifth of June 1944, when Rome had been freed by the Allies, she told him what Pietro and Ada had known—how in fact she had gotten the children.

He went with Giulia to look for their mother, but there wasn't any news of her, and it was only her sister they found. She had been hidden under a staircase all eight months, by people who had never known her till they saw her fleeing the German trucks.

It was clear that Franco remembered his aunt. Formally, as if finishing a ritual, Giulia placed the younger child in the woman's arms, saying simply, "Aldo." As solemnly, she delivered the hand of the older one, saying, "Franco."

That it was this particular girl who entered
my life cannot have been purely chance. It is too
much coincidence, and I must reconsider everything.

I've never spoken of you, Don Viale, nor of
course have I mentioned Claudine, though once
I almost did. It was long ago, still in Italy, when
I had written one of that series of letters to you
and Claudine.

Carissimo Don Viale,
. . . I know that you will be informed. When you
hear of anything, please, tell me. You told me not to
delude myself, I know, but it isn't possible for me to
live without some hope. I'm enclosing a letter. Please,
hold it until you can give or send it to her. . . .

My darling Claudine,
. . . Forgive me if you can. Or if not, try to understand. The moment was over before I could think.
My brother was tortured, and I—put to the test—
was paralyzed with fear. I was a coward, but I beg
you, let Don Viale plead for me.

Carissimo Don Viale,
. . . Even if she can forgive me, I know she will
never be able to love me. I've decided to marry. The
girl is like one of the people to whom you entrusted
Claudine—a child of peasants, with five years of
schooling, who had nothing but her life and the
strength that I, in spite of all of my advantages,
didn't have. . . .

. . . Don Viale,
. . . I, if anyone, can know of the pain you feel for
the death of her child, but since there is, in fact, a
woman among the survivors, perhaps it's Claudine. . . .

. . . Don Viale,
Forgive me for my recent letter. You must think
that I, already twenty-three, am either a stupid boy
or the worst of men. I was thinking of only the one I
love, and not of others, for whom your sorrow is—as
it ought to be—as great as your sorrow would be for
Claudine. . . .

. . . Don Viale,
. . .I should have known. I didn't deserve that she
be the one who survived. . . .

. . . Don Viale,
. . . I'll go mad. The pictures of the camps are driving me mad . . . I could have saved her child. . .

. . . Don Viale,
. . . I have nightmares and worse—murderous day-
time rages—and Giulia bears the brunt of them. Nor
can I explain. I'd have to admit to her what I had
done—what I *hadn't* done—and I couldn't bear to
face her contempt. I am cut off even from Giulia. . . .

My darling Claudine,
People would say I'm a madman, writing to a

woman who is dead. But I have to reach you—somehow. I must by some symbolic, appropriate action join you, as Don Viale was joined to a personal God by his vows. It's you who will keep me living and sane, as union with God has kept Don Viale living and sane in a monstrous, nightmarish world.

This letter to Claudine, however, he didn't mail. He crumpled it into a ball which he cupped in one of his hands. Then he struck a match and—in his upturned palm, which was an altar—set the letter aflame, and held it until it had turned to ash.

Since then, Don Viale, I've felt myself joined to Claudine and have shut that part of my past away from my wife. She, until now, has allowed it, but she was beside me today when I saw the child—when indeed I *grasped* the child—and I think she no longer will. And I find I'm asking myself: has it been my bond with Claudine that has kept me sane, or equally my bond with Giulia? Was today's coincidence meant as a sign—a warning—to help me avert a second loss? Is that why the child was put in my path?

I will tell you something else, dear friend—because it's only to you that I would admit this—that I harbor a little resentment toward Giulia. Her courage when she took the children was the courage of inexperience, of her not having known the price she'd have paid were she caught. And this innocence—though I'm ashamed to admit that I think this—diminishes,

in my eyes, what she achieved, and makes her
victory a somewhat cheap one, so that I find I'm
resentful at times of the peace that she won.

Perhaps I ought to erase that admission, but if
I let it stand, perhaps you will have some respect
for me nevertheless. I have a wife, a son and a
cherished grandson, and yet I am today desper-
ately alone and afraid. My very dear friend,
write to me, please.

He sealed and addressed the envelope and put it into his
coat. Then he wrote another letter:

My faithful Claudine,
I saw your child.

When they opened the door to the room, Vincent was still
at the desk. There was an odor of something burnt, and
Julia gasped, rushed to Vincent and lifted his hand. Then
she went to the bed and sat down, helpless and bent.

"He's done it again. He's suffering, Raymond, help him."

"Done what?"

"Look at his hand."

Raymond went to the desk. "My God, did you do it on
purpose?" He snatched the ice-cube bucket and ran to the
door, calling, "Get out of here, Chris, go back to our room."

Chris remained where he was, unwilling to leave but
afraid to look at his grandfather's hand.

"Chris," Vincent said, "please go down to your room."

Julia suddenly sat erect. "No, he's staying—he isn't a
child."

"You're happy seeing him hurt?"

"He's been hurt much worse. He knows how to cope."

"Chris," he said, quietly, "I want you to go."

"Then when Raymond gets back," she said, "Raymond goes too. You can't have Raymond if I can't have Chris."

Raymond was back and running some water over the ice. He rushed to the desk and plunged his father's hand into the bucket.

"Why did you *do* it?"

Quietly, Vincent answered, "Forget it."

Raymond turned to Julia. "For God's sake, *tell* me."

"He writes a letter—he hasn't done it in years—he holds it and sets it afire." Chris's hand shot to the side of his head. "Now *everyone* knows," Julia said, "and after today on the street, for *his* sake more than for mine—*he's* the one who knows why he's doing it—ask!"

Raymond turned. "Yes! You're going to have to tell me, Dad, or I'll see that you tell it to somebody else."

"Raymond, remember?" Vincent asked. "When you told us Kate had left you, and we asked you why, you said, 'It's private, just between Kate and me.' And later when you told us, 'She doesn't want Chris—he's coming with *me*,' and we said, 'How can she not want Chris?' you answered, 'That's private too.' "

"I see," Raymond said, "you're saying you remember every single word, and now you're paying me back."

"No. Reminding you that what applies to you applies to me."

"But it isn't the same! You say that *Mom* is irrational going to *church*."

"All right, I know. This was the last time."

"What does *that* mean? Are you planning something worse?"

"Wait a minute, Raymond." Julia said. "Vincent, when you said 'private' just between Raymond and Kate, did you mean that this burning your hand is private too, but between *us?* Because of something maybe *I* did?"

"Mom, stop it!" Raymond said. "Let me talk to him— you wanted me to talk to him, didn't you?" And turning to Vincent again, he asked, "What did you mean by 'the last time'?"

"Raymond, enough. I promised it's over. Just take Chris and leave us awhile."

Julia nodded, aware she had won—something, at least— that if Chris had to go, Raymond went too.

But Raymond, as if in rebellion, sat down. Then, thinking it over, he stood up and went back to the desk. "Can I help with your hand?" he asked, and when Vincent shook his head, "What about Chris? Do we cancel his plans?"

"No. I just need some time."

"Then whenever you're ready to go again, call." He turned to the door, followed by Chris, and was gone.

Julia watched from the bed as Vincent treated his burns. "So the kit comes in handy," she said. "When we'd go on vacation you'd empty the medicine chest into that kit." She waited. "Vincent?" she asked. "Did you talk about Kate for a reason? To say that what's important is to keep from hurting *Chris?* That if Chris weren't here you'd talk?"

"No."

She waited again and watched until he had wrapped his hand and was putting the kit in a drawer.

"Vincent?" she asked. "Is Don Viale dead?"

He spun around as if caught in some terrible act. Aware

she was watching him calmly, calculatingly, in a way that was alien to her, he squared his shoulders, sat down again and faced her, silent.

Incredulous, she said, "You can't even ask how I know his name?"

"How?" he asked.

Pacified, she answered, 'I saw it on an envelope."

"Recently?"

"No."

"When?"

"Who remembers? I know you got a letter from him once that you wouldn't show me—I saw it before you saw it yourself. But the envelope I mean you were sending off to *him*. It was after your nightmares had stopped, in Rome, when you used to write letters to someone and not let me know who it was. I suspected you were writing to a woman, so once—you left the letter and went for your coat—I looked. And it wasn't to a woman but a priest. A Raimondo Viale. Is he the Raimondo that Raymond is named for?"

She studied him, wondering whether, if they were young, she would submit to this game.

"Vincent?" she asked. "Did you really mean what you said to Raymond? That you weren't paying him back? Because you know? After all these years it hurts me still, how he brushed us off when he told us 'it's private'. And never has given a clue to why they split up. Maybe if he'd confided in *us*—any bit of it—I'd find it easier talking to *him*. Wouldn't *you?* I mean he's our son after all, and my God he's given us Chris."

Vincent sighed, put off-guard by the mention of Chris. "I don't know, Julia, I really don't think so."

She thought for a while.

"Vincent? Raymond didn't let you answer the question I asked. Are you paying me back for something that *I* did?"

"You?" He shook his head. "What could *you* have done?"

"I was a whore for the Germans."

"Julia, don't act stupid."

"See?" she said. "Still an Italian! Did you ever say that Chris is stupid? Or Raymond? Me! A woman! So you can call me stupid."

"I'm sorry."

"After all the years I went to school here, everything I studied so that educated Vincent wouldn't be ashamed of peasant Julia, still you consider me stupid."

"I *told* you I'm sorry, I *never* considered you stupid, I don't even know why I said it."

She sat even taller now on the bed, watching him. He was no longer facing her. His chin was on his chest, his forehead in the hand he hadn't hurt.

"Vincent?" she said. "I was."

"You were what?"

"I just told you."

He lifted his face and waved his hand in dismissal. "You were a virgin. You were so frightened it took us a week."

"But not frightened because of inexperience, the way you thought. I worshipped you—and thought of myself as defiled."

Slowly, his face turned solemn. His eyes darkened, and he lurched forward, his body bent in place over the chair as if he were going to spring.

"No!" she shouted, "No!"—in a rage equal to his. And soon, quietly, "So that Franco and Aldo would live."

He seemed suspended by shock, and then a wildness

appeared in his eyes—the look she hadn't seen in him since years ago when he would awaken from nightmares he wouldn't reveal. He hovered over the chair, and then there was another movement of his body, a slow despairing fall, backward, down, to the shelter of the upholstered arm-chair, as he understood it all and knew her victory had not been cheap.

The moment of madness had gone, and now as in the past, wretched, he bent his body forward, his head in line with his knees and covered over with both of his hands. She fought the impulse to go to him and hold him. Instead she turned away. The strength with which she had chal-lenged him left her, and she was grieving again, just as after the sight of his hand.

Softly she said, "I thought I'd really tricked them. But the next night, there they were—three of them—the one who'd been at the desk and another two. Without the Ital-ian interpreter now—they didn't need him for this. Laugh-ing at me, an ignorant girl with her two 'illegitimate' kids. They lifted the babies off of the bed. Tore off their clothes. They made these threatening motions, as if they were chopping them off."

She paused and remembered an earlier scene, and quickly regained her strength. She lifted her head. Her eyes were looking forward, through and beyond the wall to a place that was far away and visible still.

"There was another janitor taken that night, an older woman. She was next in line at the desk, right after me. I had to bend down to Franco—I thought he would cry or look back—so I heard what she said. Someone—I don't know when—had brought her a Jewish orphan. 'He was entrusted to me,' she said. The interpreter thought she was

crazy. He kept saying, '*You* can go free. *You* are an Aryan—
like *her*, like *her*,'—pointing to me. But she stayed with the
boy. *We* at least lived, but the price? I told you. And in
front of the children, so I couldn't cry. They would come
at night—one or two or all three. One of them, if I wasn't
satisfactory, he'd hold me up in the air by my hair." She
ran her fingers across her forehead, under her hairline. "And
later, I couldn't tell you. I was sure if you knew, you'd
leave me. A peasant? Okay. But not a whore."

Tears sprang to her eyes. She had lived with Vincent far
too long and known him far too well to still believe he'd
have left her then. Nor did she think, as she recalled the
last few minutes, that his anger at her, when he had hovered over the chair, had lasted more than the moments he'd
needed to grasp the rest of what she had said. Nor did she
want their marriage to end. And yet, she would not go
back to the life they had lived in the past. That was a price
she would not accept.

She didn't turn toward Vincent or know that he had not
looked up. He remained as he had been, with even his
injured hand pressing the top of his head. In a little while,
however, he got to his feet and slowly went to her side,
near the bed.

"Giulia," he said, but she didn't respond to either his
presence or how he pronounced the "a" of her name—in
an almost forgotten way—the full Italian "a," unlike the
clipped American "a" of "Julia."

Her head was bent, and her eyes were fixed on the floor.
All he could see of her head was her hair, graying, short,
and stylishly cut. He lifted his hand and stroked it, and
stroked it again, for the nights when her weight had been
hung from it, and again, for the people who had saved the

babies' aunt, and again, for the "Aryan" janitor who had not abandoned the Jewish boy, and again, for Don Viale—struck down in the road by the Fascists' truck—and again, for his brother's severed flesh, and again and again till she showed she was fully aware of him by turning her head—not away from him but toward him. And again he stroked her hair, and found he was saying, *"Non piangere più, piccina, non piangere,"* for the second time that day.